# VICTIMS

## A HORROR SHORT STORY COLLECTION

BY
DEREK BARTON
BRIAN GATTI
& T.D. BARTON

VICTIMS: A HORROR SHORT STORY COLLECTION
© 2024 Derek Barton, Brian Gatti & T.D. Barton

All Rights Reserved. No part of this publication may be reproduced or transmitted in any form or by any means, electronic or mechanical, including photocopy, recording or any other information storage and retrieval system, without prior permission in writing from the author, except in the case of brief quotations embodied in critical reviews and certain other noncommercial uses permitted by copyright law. For permission requests, write to the author, addressed "Attention: Permissions Coordinator," at the email address below:

Rivyenphx@gmail.com

All rights reserved.

ISBN Ebook: TBD

The authors Derek Barton, Brian Gatti, and T.D. Barton have asserted their rights under the Copyright, Designs and Patents Act, 1988 to be identified as the authors of this work.

This is a work of fiction. The characters in it are all fiction. Resemblance to any persons living or dead is purely coincidental. Some liberties have been taken with a few building locations and descriptions. Names, characters, places and incidents either are the products of the author's imagination or are used fictitiously.

# CONTENTS

WHEELS ON THE BUS....5
VICTIM ONE....13
DIY BRAINWASHING....19
THE PIPE DREAM....36
PORTRAIT OF A KILLER....43
LATE NIGHT DINNER GUESTS....56
THE LONG STRETCH....67
THERE'S SOMETHING IN THE BASEMENT....75
THE BOOK OF I....107
ISOLATED....127
THE CYCLE....143
TENTH....153
BROTHERS....166
TIP LINE....178
IT GROWLS FROM THE CORNER....198

**BLIGHT HOTEL....209

THE WHEELS ON THE BUS                    BY DEREK BARTON


## 2:38 AM.

It was the beginning of the hard hours. The hours of 2:00 to 4:00 AM are when the ghosts in my head shout the loudest. Sometimes they screamed at me. Sometimes at each other. Or hell, sometimes the ghosts just wanted to scream. I guess in eternity, you have that luxury. What else are you going to do?

The pull was always there. Even in the good years after AA saved my life, the constant pull remained. It started at an early age for me. I was 8 and found the key to the liquor cabinet. The taste wasn't good at all at first. I couldn't believe that the adults drank what had to be part gasoline.

However, when the buzz hit me, the lightheadedness was awesome. I never felt anything like it. It was almost like that thrilling, out-of-control feeling you get when you are on a tall slide. Wind blowing by you, the ground approaching fast. You are helpless but at the same time, you are having an amazing experience knowing you'll be safe. This felt even better as I plopped down in the center of the kitchen floor. My head spun, my heart raced, and a great sense of joy spread over me. I continued to down the clear vodka bottle.

Anyway, I have been a bad drunk, a recovering alcoholic, a neglectful dad, and finally a hit-rock-bottom survivor in my illustrious forty-eight years of life.

I guide the puttering moped over the curb and up to the bar's entrance. Janie's Tavern has been home for a couple of months now. Her arms are always spread wide to welcome her wayward son.

The burly kid bouncer at the door gives me a nod and holds the door open for me. The music is obnoxious and loud but that's okay. It helps to cover the screaming mimies in my brain some.

"Brett, slide me over a Miller and a Wild Eagle Bourbon Chaser. It's gonna be a long night," I proclaim.

His eyebrows shoot up and he gives me a questioning look.

"Yeah, I'm sure. It's the night of a bad anniversary and I need a little support. So, hook a fella up!"

I sit at the counter. The stools are all empty. A few tables have other patrons, but in the corner, one man in a jean jacket glances in my direction. He is scruffy with a long straggly beard and greasy brown hair. He is shy of 270 pounds, but I guess the majority of his mass is in his beefy arms. Maybe at one point he had been in football or was a bodybuilder of some sort.

I nod in his direction and raise my shot glass in a friendly salute to him.

He smiles and lifts up his tall glass of beer.

I take a deep breath. I haven't been on the wagon for nearly five years, but the last three months I tried to keep it at a beer here and there.

Tonight, I was throwing out that rule.

I threw back the shot and felt its fiery contents delightfully burn as they worked their way down.

"And let's not let the poor fella be lonely down there, Brett. Another shot, please!"

"Whoa, easy man. Are you celebrating tonight?" Said the man in the jean jacket. He suddenly stood behind me. Must've walked up as I drank and was still nursing his drink.

"No. Not celebrating, but tonight is five years to the day of... to the day of a morning that no one could ever believe."

I got quiet. The shouting in my head eased back but this left the stage open for the child whispers that were far worse for me.

*When are we going to get there, Mister Donner?*

*What time is it? Are we running late, sir?*

*Can we go back? I left my homework for Miss Janda's class.*

*I have to go potty, Mister Donner. Are we there yet?*

*What's that? Is someone on the road?*

That last one. That voice in particular was little Susie. Her tiny, high-pitched but sweet voice cried out. The last question she ever said. I hear it over and over in my nightmares. A simple, innocent question.

*By gods, where was she? Where were they?*

"You okay there, pal?" The man asked as he eased down on the stool next to me.

"Uh, yeah, sorry. Lost in here," I said as I poked my index finger into the side of my temple.

He extended his hand. "Gary. Yours?"

"Charlie," I lied.

"Sounds like you have a doozy of a story. Can you spill it? Or are you a secret agent on a classified mission?"

I laughed hard at his joke. Laughed too hard and too long, drawing stares, but the drinks were already affecting me.

"Sorry. Yeah, it's a weird story." I paused and stared at him. He was drinking his beer and now starting to light up a Maverick Cigarette. His finger had a white tan line where a possible wedding ring was missing.

"It's not a happy ending. You sure you are in the right mood for it, Gary?"

"I love stories. Come on, quit stalling."

I motioned to the bartender one more time. More liquid courage.

After I finished the shot and splashed more beer to follow it, I opened up, climbed over the mental wall I built up, and relived the worst morning of my life.

"It was... well, I am not going to say what town, but it was your typical small town. I was driving the #237 for this Elementary School. I just passed Munroe Street after grabbing that chubby Darryl Sampson kid. The brat always left wrappers in the backseat and chocolate smears on the seats. Anyway, it was the last of the loop. Now it was time to head to the school lot for the drop-off.

"Traffic had been light. Even holiday light you might say, but it was a normal weekday. I went down Jefferson and made a left to take Lawson Avenue to the Torv Tunnel.

"I noticed right away that there were no lights inside, and it was unusually dark. When we entered and as I reached for my headlights, a stupid sedan, maybe a Prius, nearly swiped my left wheel. It cut across and sped ahead. I had to brake hard and turn the bus into the gravel at the side.

"'Hold on, kids. Hold on!' I shouted as we bumped and bounced along.

"I was instantly hot. I hate bad drivers. Got a bit of that road rage bug, you know.

"I heard lots of screams and shouts at first from the kids as expected, but it was Susie Willey's question that cut through all the chaos.

"*'What's that? Is someone on the road?'*

"I saw only the thick curtain of darkness ahead and the patch of roadway lit before the bus. No one was there. Not even that damn sedan. That asshat must've kept driving and went further into the tunnel.

"I ground the bus to a stop. 'It's okay, kids. Nothing to worry about. Everyone okay?'

"Not a sound.

"I shot a glance up to the overhead rearview mirror. No one was back there! They were just...gone."

I waited for Gary's shout of 'That's bullshit!" but he only stared back at me. His mouth was open and slack-jawed. His drink sat abandoned on the bar. His cigarette was nearly done and smoldering in his hand.

"What? They were gone. What do you mean?" Gary asked.

I waited to see the building suspicion on his face. For five years now, I have seen it often. It goes from shock, disbelief, and suspicion to outright anger. Sometimes it goes right to distrust and hate.

"I know how it sounds. But, yeah, no one was on the bus but me. Their bags were still there, their little lunch pails, and water thermoses, but no kids. I couldn't fathom what happened and where they went.

"I ran up the aisle in pure panic. I looked out the side windows, but the tunnel was dark and quiet.

"I pulled out my cell phone, but it took me a moment to figure out who to call. What do I even say? What would they understand? What would they believe? 'All the kids just vanished. Poof!'" I shrugged and took another long sip from my fourth beer. My body growing numb from the alcohol.

"The police arrived in seconds. A busload of children goes missing, including the mayor's own two sons, that gets you their immediate attention!

"As they scoured the bus for any signs of foul play, they took me back to headquarters. I spent the next forty-eight hours in constant interrogation rooms, explaining what I saw over and over. They refused to listen or to give me any credit."

Gary cut in. "Did you really think they would buy that? You were the last adult with them."

"I know. But, I have been a good driver for that school for six years, not a single complaint or problem. I hadn't drunk a sip of any beer or alcohol in all that time. I was good man, good. I told the truth—"

"That's all that happened? You aren't leaving anything out?"

He was starting to upset me.

"No! All they saw was some freak, a psycho that abducted a lot of kids and did God-knows-what with them. Wouldn't accept that I didn't know. Finally, after the forty-eight-hour hold, my public defender got me released without any charges. They had nothing, they knew nothing. I knew nothing. They wasted time on me when they could have found those kids!"

Brett was at the other end of the bar and cleaning out the ice machine. "Wow. No charges?" he asked.

I nodded. "Didn't stop the press, man. Didn't stop their smear campaign. Suddenly, I was public enemy number one. A raging lunatic, drunk dad, and overall, must've been a 'closet molester'. Every detail of my life was scrutinized, judged, and blasted out for all to know. Would anyone look good after that?"

Gary continued to listen, smoke, and soak in every word. He didn't seem to be getting worked up and wasn't passing judgment. At least not yet.

"So, what did you finally do? What happened?"

"Can I have one of those?" I pointed to the pack on the bar. He slipped a cigarette out, lit it, and waited for my story to continue.

"I left town after only two weeks. I was getting death threat calls at night. Someone took a bat to my car, and another threw a brick in the front window. More than anything, I couldn't take the looks. I left and started using my middle name. Then that didn't work. I was found. I was stalked by some lowlife reporter in the neighboring town.

"So, I packed up and went way West. They have never found me again, but...they never found them kids either. I hate that they never got an answer to that. And I'm sure it didn't look good - the main suspect in a case with over a dozen kids missing, up and flees.

"What could I tell them, the police, the parents? I didn't do anything. I didn't see anything. I don't know how to find those kids."

"Man... So, the police didn't find anything?"

"No. At least I don't think so. They wouldn't share information with me, of course." I took a large gulp of the beer. "Brett, get me two more shots. I have had five years of this shit and I have earned five shots."

Gary laughed and lit up another cigarette as I hammered the shots. It was near closing and only the three of us remained.

He held out his hand. "Bud, I think you should let me take you home. Hand over your keys."

"Shit, man, I only have a scooter. Lost my license long ago."

"Oh," Gary said and glanced at Brett, looking irritated. He then sighed loudly as he looked down at his glass. I wondered if that was the same beer all this time.

"Then I guess we should call it a night, Roy."

I snapped a look at him. *He knew my real name!*

Gary leaned in close to my face. "You don't recognize me, do you?"

I could only stare in silence.

He pointed at the bartender. "That is Brett Sampson, and I am his brother, Gary Sampson! You know, little brat, Daryl Sampson's uncle and father!" Brett pulled out a wooden bat from under the bar.

Vomit started to rise in my throat, but Gary's meaty hands wrapped around it too fast. He slammed me to the floor, choking and crushing me. He screamed, "WHERE IS MY BOY, YOU BASTARD? GIVE HIM BACK! GIVE HIM BACK!"

My lungs burned. I gasped and gulped for air without success. He loosened his hands to plunge his thumbnails into my eyes. He wanted blood and he plumbed my skull for it. I felt sharp pangs of pain as Brett's bat hammered into my rib cage. Gary lifted my head from the sticky floor and began slamming my head again and again into the wood.

"NO ONE BELIEVES YOUR SHIT STORY! WHERE ARE THEY? WHAT DID YOU DO, YOU PERVERT?" Brett roared.

I heard Gary Sampson howl in pure anger and fury one last time as he blasted the back of my head into–

VICTIM ONE  BY DEREK BARTON

A brutal windstorm had blown up out of nowhere. The weatherman on the radio stated, "Tonight a severe thunderstorm has crossed into the valley. Please take shelter immediately. In my personal opinion, folks, in my fifteen years of broadcasting here in Chicago, I haven't seen a storm like this suddenly appear and have this much power. I urge everyone off the streets! Take your Treaters home now. Candy, after all, can be bought at the store!"

His rant was cut off by abrupt static and then the station began an oldie, *Little Red Riding Hood* by Sam the Sham and The Pharaohs.

Sheila looked in her rearview mirror and spotted Rascal. The red Doberman was nestled among her plastic bags. They contained her last-minute supplies for Brayden's Halloween costume. Some glue, white cotton, red ribbon spools, and a kit of creme paints. She bent down to turn on her cell phone. It read, "4:55 PM".

*Damn,* she fretted. *I only have an hour or so to put this together! Gary's coming from work so maybe he'll be late to pick him up.*

"Even bad wolves can be good..." she sang along with the radio. "Is that true boy?" She laughed as Rascal only yawned in response.

As she crossed the center lane and turned onto I-57, large bullets of rain pelted her window. The storm fresh off of Lake Michigan picked up in its intensity. Crazy rolling thunderheads billowed and blew overhead. It grew prematurely dark outside.

Her fingers strummed along subconsciously on the steering wheel with the tune. The air inside became humid and somewhat stale as she had the Camry's heater turned off.

A high-pitched horn pierced her thoughts. Sheila cranked the wheel to the right on instinct as a red pickup zoomed past narrowly missing her. The driver cursed and waved his fist at her. Sheila had obviously pulled out into his lane. Rascal barked from the back seat, scratching at the window.

"Sorry. So sorry!" she squealed out loud, but, of course, the truck had already gone down the highway. Shaking at his reaction and the near collision, she pulled over into the breakdown lane to settle herself.

"It's not my fault. Right, boy? The storm is clouding everything. And I have no time to delay!"

Not too close behind her, she spied a set of headlights pull into the breakdown lane and park.

"SEE! Other people are having a hard time too." She said in defense. Rascal whined in sympathy.

She stretched out her arms, one hand scratching him behind the ear, and she shook her whole frame one last time. She felt ready so she drove the car back onto the road.

On the freeway, the speed limit was 65 max, but no one except the elderly drove that limit. She quickly passed 65 to nudge it closer to 75. There were few other drivers on the road and the drive was smooth again. The radio began a new tune, *Sitting on the Dock of the Bay.*

She hummed again and began to enjoy the ride. Exit 78 passed by, marking the border to the small burg called Oak Forest. She smiled to herself in relief. *Only 3 more exits then I'll be inside. Maybe a cup of French Roast?*

"How about a couple of strips of maple bacon, Rascal? Would that make it up to you? Dragging you out in-"

Red and blue lights splashed all over the interior of the Camry. Her eyes darted to the rearview. A police cruiser was behind her with its lights whirling. Her eyes went next to the dashboard. It showed 79. *Not too much over, not normally worth hassling* me, she thought.

*But it is raining pretty hard...*

With no other cars near her, she had no issues getting the vehicle pulled over to the side. She parked, turned off the car, and leaned over to dig in the glove department.

"DRIVER STOP MOVING. PLACE YOUR HANDS ON THE STEERING WHEEL IMMEDIATELY!" The booming voice came through the cruiser's speakers.

She froze, shocked by the fierce tone of the voice.

"DRIVER STOP MOVING! SIT UP AND PLACE YOUR HANDS ON THE WHEEL! I AM NOT GOING TO GIVE YOU ANOTHER WARNING!" The voice was masculine, aggressive, and agitated.

"Okay, okay!" she said out loud. Rascal pounced around the Halloween packages and whined again in excitement. She sat still behind the wheel with her hands at the 10 and 2 positions.

A long minute went by and finally, a shadowy figure emerged from the cruiser. It was a man, all alone. Tall with broad shoulders, a hat, and a gray rain poncho. He slowly advanced, checked the license plate, then lit up the backseat with his flashlight. Rascal went berserk until she yelled for him to stop.

*Come on, come on. You're killing me! I have to get Brayden's costume done. For god sakes, just write me up, and let's go already!* Sheila's thoughts cascaded around and around.

He tapped at the window with the butt of the flashlight. She hit the button and rolled it down halfway. Rain splattered her immediately.

She looked up but could only see angular shadows and a faint highlight of his face. Wide nose, far-spaced eyes, and a bushy beard. She noted the fact his mouth was in a deep scowl.

"Sorry, Officer, to make you stand in the rain." She muttered, trying to be charming and get on his good side. "And don't worry about Rascal. He's too old for a fight."

"All part of the job. License and registration, please." He ignored her attempt at charm. His voice was void of any humor.

As she leaned over, she noticed his hand slid over to his holster. He rested it on the top of the gun inside.

It remained there as she handed him the paperwork.

Without glancing at the papers, he said, "All right, Mrs. Glenn, can you step out?"

"Are you serious? Is that really necessary?"

He took a large step back from her door. Rested his hand again on the leather holster on his belt. "Step out! I do not like to repeat my orders, Mrs. Glenn!"

She sighed softly, more to herself than as a protest. She didn't like his tone and demeanor. She understood he wasn't to be pushed.

More rain flooded the interior as she got out. Rascal whimpered and then emitted a low growl. The storm itself took advantage of her appearance and increased in its fury.

He slipped a hand around her forearm and led her to the back of her car with a firm grip.

"I am going to have to pat you down now. Any sharp items or weapons on you I need to be aware of?"

She shook her head no as his hands roughly went over her shoulders and then down her sides. He removed her wallet and car keys from her jeans pocket. She wasn't wearing a jacket, so she carried nothing else upon her.

"What is this all about exactly?" She cried out over the storm's cacophony.

He seized her left arm and yanked it painfully high between her shoulders. Her breath blasted from her lungs as he bent her over the hood. She heard the sound of the metal handcuffs as they clicked shut on her wrists. Then his heavy body lay on top of her. He was smothering her against her own car!

Leaning into her ear, he said, "Your husband, Gary, says he is sick of you not being there for him or your son. Now, you will never be."

He lifted off. At the same time, threw a very heavy punch into her ribs, then kicked her hip with his boot to knock her to the ground. As she wheezed and writhed on the ground, he popped open the trunk of her car. Dimly, she heard the sound of furious dog barking.

The officer scooped her into his arms and threw her like a bag of trash into the trunk. The rain ramped up once again and all sounds were drowned out by the pounding flurry.

Panic seized her, but she couldn't decide how to act. Her fight-or-flight instincts overwhelmed her, and he kept taking action before she could decide. He was calm, precise, and calculated.

*Oh God! This is routine for him! He's practiced this!*

He bent down close to her face. He had bright green eyes, one though was all bloody from a burst blood vessel. His breath smelled equal parts Scope Mint and Buffalo Trace Bourbon. Her Dad drank it often.

"A parting gift from me," he said as he showed her a long, black plastic zip tie. Sheila shrieked as he secured it around her neck.

Her final plea of "No, don't do this, please!" was shut off as he tightened the zip tie. It bit into the skin and blood bubbled up around it as she clawed at it frantically. Her eyes bulged and her tongue stuck out obscenely.

He muttered to himself, "I am doing it. I'm getting my first! I am doing it!"

It was over in seconds, but to Sheila, it seemed endless before her vision faded, the colors blending then going gray, and finally dissolving to an infinite black. The whole time the man bounced from one foot to the other. He continued his stream of words, "I am getting my first. I am getting my first. Yes! All I planned. Precise. *So easy...*"

Hours later, a group of teens "too old for Trick-or-Treating" found Shelia's empty car abandoned along an isolated dirt road. It was a minor inferno, smoke rising and bleeding into the clouds when the local fire department arrived. Her remains did not take long to discover.

Mysteriously, one backdoor to the empty backseats was left open, facing the surrounding forest.

*DIY BRAINWASHING*             *BY BRIAN GATTI*

Phase 0 - Commit to You

The doorbell chimed, and Paulette looked up as she absently petted a calico cat. "Welcome to Cozy Cats!" she called out with a smile to the tall brunette who walked in. The woman flashed a friendly smile before heading to a table where another woman sat.

A commotion erupted from the Parapsychology and Religion section as an awkwardly slender young man with golden curly hair rushed out, chasing a pillow-shaped tabby carrying a croissant.

Paulette raised her eyebrows with amusement and said, "Everything ok, Damon?" He glanced at her before lunging downward, his left hand catching the cat while the right removed the pastry.

Straightening himself with dignity, Damon glanced scornfully at the angry cat. "Yes. Baroness Bastet Chubbs, the third of her name, resented her vet-imposed diet and stole a customer's croissant." He paused, looking at the mangled food with disappointment in his green eyes. "My croissant."

Paulette grinned and said, "Why not set that aside for the birds and get yourself a new one? Oh! I have a new haiku." With a shyness she hated but never could get past when talking to him, she said, "I wrote a new haiku for the board." She slid it across the counter.

With a look of genuine delight, Damon set the croissant down on the counter. As he reached for the paper, Baroness Bastet Chubbs- the third of her name - moved with the speed and stealth one would not expect from a cat shaped like a throw pillow and stole the unattended pastry. Damon sighed with defeat and shook his head, sharing a grin with Paulette before he lifted the sheet.

"Attention, patrons, and residents of Cozy Cat Cafe and Bookstore! We have a new catku, a kitty-focused haiku from our talented leader!" Damon's voice shifted from its usual soft tone to that of a circus ringmaster announcing the show as he gestured towards Paulette.

Paulette shook her head, taking it in stride as Damon smiled at her. The customers paused their conversations and shopping; the only sound was

Baroness Bastet tearing into the croissant. Damon cleared his throat and said, "An Ode Petey. Orange and white delight, your silly games bring us joy; who's the best kitty?"

Everyone laughed and clapped politely. Damon grinned at her playfully and then said, "I'll get this on the chalkboard outside and then make your uncle's tea."

\* \* \*

Several hours later, Paulette arrived at her uncle's manor. A servant let her in and showed her upstairs. She hesitantly approached her uncle's office door, hand poised to knock. Uncle Paul's health had been declining fast, and she knew the end was near. She held back for several seconds, steeling herself. Her uncle was one of the few people in her life who seemed to truly love her and accept her unremarkable self, which seemed so odd to her, considering how remarkable his life was with his wealth and many business interests.

She released a slow breath and knocked on the wooden door. There was a moment's delay when he answered, still strong despite the ravages of lung cancer, "Please, my dear, come in."

Paulette opened the door and stepped into her uncle's office, a fascinating collection of artifacts from a well-lived life - paintings, sculptures, and trinkets all arranged artfully but also with a sense of disregard, as though lacking the care one might use to show beloved treasures.

Uncle Paul sat near the fireplace, wearing a comfortable charcoal gray suit that hung awkwardly on his skeletal frame. Once a large man, the cancer had diminished him to the point where he was almost unrecognizable. Only the stern silver blue eyes seemed the same, buried in his haggard face, as though they were trapped. A cigarette dangled from the right side of his mouth, which he removed and set down in the gold ashtray.

She quieted a shiver as she approached, finding his illness-riddled appearance unsettling. He attempted to stand as she walked to him, but his legs were insufficient for the task; they wobbled briefly before he dropped back down.

"Please stay, Uncle," she said as she approached him, leaning down to kiss his beard-bristled cheek. She glanced down at the cigarette, lip curled in disgust. "Why are you smoking? It can't help."

"Yes, yes," he replied irritably, even as he smiled at the kiss. "Seeing as how the cancer is already killing this wretched body, I can't see how more can hurt." Next to him was a bowl of peanuts covered in red powder and a table with a chess board with the white pieces facing the empty chair. "Come sit. We have a lot to discuss, and I don't know how long I can stay before I need my medicine..." the words choked off with violent coughing, fine flecks of blood sprayed the board.

Paulette reached for a handkerchief to wipe it, but he waved her away. "Thomas can do it later," he gasped, his eyes watering as he struggled to catch his breath. She set the tea down before him. Damon's special blend of herbs should help."

Paulette remained quiet as her uncle tried to control his labored breathing; each inhalation brought a new grimace of pain. The wet sound of his efforts was accompanied by the crackle of the fire and the relentless rain on the window, tapping impatiently for the old man's death.

"Ah yes, your little cat hobby. How silly," he said in that infuriating, dismissive tone when discussing her business. "You're looking rounder. Did you add more pastries to the menu?"

She grinned tightly at this and shook her head.

When his breathing calmed, he said, "The worst part about dying is how long it takes." He grinned, blood showing on his teeth. Uncle Paul sipped the tea she brought and winced at the flavor. He swallowed the hot liquid quickly, finishing it. "Thank him for me. It may taste like shit, but it helps. Speaking of things that taste like shit," his words trailed off, picked up the bowl of nuts, and put it on the chessboard, popping a few in his mouth and chewing.

Paulette picked a red-stained peanut off the pile and chewed slowly, savoring the familiar salty flavor mixed with the heat from ground spices. It was something he'd created decades ago during a culinary phase, and somehow, it stuck despite not being very good. The thought of never having a moment like this again made her eyes water.

"Uncle, what are these covered in? I've been asking since I was twelve, but now that you're dying, can you tell me?" It was her favorite game with him, and he'd always tell her something fantastical, though now the joy was tainted by the acknowledgment of the impending tragedy.

"It has magical herbs, but the secret ingredient is my blood." He laughed hoarsely and ate another nut before offering her one.

"Your blood? That's new. To being immortal vampires then." She said, raising a nut in a mock toast before chewing it. "Speaking of mortality, how are you doing? Besides the obvious."

"I'm ok. I'm not afraid to die. I'm looking forward to what's next. I'm tired of this broken body. Unfortunately, this vessel is too fragile to hold all life has to offer," Uncle Paul said as he touched her hand.

Paulette smiled tightly at this, understanding his desire to end his pain. Her uncle was the only one who ever really noticed her, and as the pain of anticipated loss built up like hot coals in her chest, she let herself cry; her red-rimmed eyes focused on his weathered face. "I know. I'm just so sad. I'm going to miss you, Uncle Paul. I love you so much. You don't deserve to die."

He grasped her hand with surprising strength and whispered fiercely, "I'll never be gone. I'll be in your heart and your mind." Uncle Paul grinned and released her fingers, motioning to the nuts. "You'll have plenty of Uncle Paul's Rusty Nuts to keep you company; there's a special batch waiting with your inheritance. To remember me. Hopefully, you won't go through them so quickly."

She grinned weakly and ate another, savoring the familiar and bitter flavor like a treasured memory of pain. "I know. I know." Paulette looked away, tears filling her eyes.

Uncle Paul wiped at her tears and said, "I don't have much time left. I have a few things to tell you. Are you listening? Really listening?"

Paulette nodded.

"First, you are the most important person in my life. You always have been. I may not always be kind, but it's for your good. You are meant for greater things." He grinned as she looked up in shock. "Second, I am gifting you something very important: a videotape that helped me transform my life when I was your age. Last, I know you're unhappy. I need you to commit, Paulette. I need you to commit to changing things for yourself to become your best self. Can you give me that?"

Paulette swallowed the lump in her throat as she nodded, fresh tears falling.

"You need to say it. Say, I commit to changing myself."

"I-I commit to changing myself," she stuttered, shocked at his vehemence.

"Very good. Here's the other piece. Your parents and siblings will receive five million each, fair compensation, I think, for what they've given me. The rest will be held in trust for you." Uncle Paul's eyes locked on her as he spoke, his voice strangely intense. "That will give you approximately one hundred twenty million in assets, including this house, but with some conditions."

A nut fell from Paulette's hand to the table, shock etched on her face. "What?"

"You are unsculpted clay, full of unrealized potential. I want you to find your purpose. And when you do, the money will be yours."

"Why?" Paulette managed, fighting through the shock. "Why me?"

"Because you're the only one who truly matters and can carry on my legacy. The tape gave me the keys to my success. It'll help you do the same. You need to watch it. Do you understand?"

"Yes," she began, but her voice made it clear she didn't mean it. "Compensation for what?"

Uncle Paul didn't answer. Instead, his face relaxed, and he said, "You're a good kid. You deserve better." Uncle Paul coughed and wiped blood from his lips. "You best go; I need to sleep now."

Phase I - Acknowledge Opportunities

Two days later, Uncle Paul died from a pulmonary embolism, a consequence of the damage to his cancer-ridden lungs. The funeral was prompt and surprisingly simple for someone of such wealth - a quiet graveside service to less than twenty people.

A week later, her family met at the lawyer's office for the will reading. While never a loving family, Paulette was shocked by their formality and coldness, as though her uncle's death ended their relationship with her, such as it was. As her uncle said, her parents and two older brothers were relatives more in name than deed due to their age difference. Each inherited five million dollars. As he promised, Paulette was bequeathed a box with a **VHS** tape, a **VHS** player, a tin of Uncle Paul's Rusty Nuts, and his last pack of cigarettes. A committed anti-smoker and someone who lost her uncle to lung cancer, she curled her nose at this but didn't comment. She'd just throw it away later.

What shocked her was that her family didn't comment at all on the box of crap or the fact that Paulette was effectively the sole heir. The lawyer explained that the assets in the trust would be released to Paulette once she completed her uncle's final wishes. They seemed resentful but refused to remark on it. As they left the lawyer's office, her father looked like he would say something to her, but her mother silenced him with an elbow to the ribs.

Since Paulette hadn't seen or touched a VCR in over fifteen years, it took twenty minutes and two YouTube videos to figure out how to use it. Dusty and aggravated by the effort, Paulette sat on her sagging tan couch and set the old cardboard box beside her. She picked up her glass of wine and sipped it as she turned on the TV. The tin of nuts lay open next to her, and she popped one in her mouth.

The dull blue input screen on her television blurred as the VCR came to life, replaced by tracking lines and static before the video began, a gray lined square with the words, DIY Brainwashing: 4 Steps to New Purpose, by Dr. Ian Temeril, copyright MCMLXXXIII.

Paulette leaned back onto the couch and sipped her wine, watching the screen as the image changed to show a man in his late eighties wearing a vomit-green suit, a yellow dress shirt, and a paisley tie that merged both colors. He sat in a high-back chair on a low-rise stage with a cigarette smoldering in his right hand.

"Hello, I am Dr. Temeril, and I'm excited to invite you on a journey of self-discovery. What's your name?"

Paulette raised her eyebrows and smirked. "What is this, Dora the Explorer? How long does he wait before pretending to hear me?"

The video remained still, save for the doctors blinking and the smoke. Awkwardly, she said, "Paulette."

Immediately, he began speaking again, "So nice to meet you. Are you ready?"

"Yes," she said, smothering self-conscious feelings with a swallow of wine. *This is ridiculous*, she thought to herself, but her uncle asked her to try, and he was obscenely successful, so why not?

"Great," the doctor said. He leaned forward in his chair, the burning cigarette hanging from the right side of his mouth, reminding her briefly of Uncle Paul. "Now, repeat after me. I am full of flaws. I am a broken vessel. Here is an account of my failure as a person. Then I want you to list your flaws."

Paulette frowned at the doctor's words and shook her head, rejecting the idea. "This is stupid. How does this help anyone?" Then, she heard her uncle's voice urging her to commit to changing and finding her purpose. With a sigh, she repeated the words. Then she looked down at herself, considering her flaws.

In a flat voice, she said, "I'm fat." Nothing happened; the words had no impact, a limp self-critique she'd told too many times to hurt anymore. The doctor just gazed at her through the video with polite disinterest. "Umm. I'm wasting time with my pointless shop. It's just cats and books. It's not even original. It could close tomorrow, and no one would cry." She shivered as the chill in her words came closer to the mark.

Her mind turned to Damon's sweet smile, which burned in her chest. "I'm alone all the time, and I'm unlovable." A sob bubbled up from her throat as the cold cruelty of her words burned her. "I'm worthless. When Uncle Paul died, people cared. When I die..." her face twisted in pain as another sob escaped. "When I die," she said, forcing strength in her voice, "no one will care. No one will miss me."

The doctor nodded; his expression seemed eager as he listened. There was a minute's delay, which she used to wipe her face, the empty pain of her admissions leaving her emotionally numb.

"Good job!" the video enthusiastically said. "How very brave of you. This is the completion of the first phase. You've uncovered and admitted your deepest flaws. Please stop the video here and write down your revelations. You may move on to Phase 2 in two days. For now, read your insights three times a day."

Then, inexplicably, the video paused, and her reflection on the screen overlaid the doctor's smiling face before she used the remote to turn the TV off.

Phase 2 - Open Yourself to Change

Deep in the night, the heavy sound of someone hammering on her apartment door disrupted Paulette's sleep. Groggily, she sat up and looked at her clock; the smeary blue numbers revealed nothing but the lateness of the hour.

She climbed out of bed as the hammering continued, grabbing her phone and dialing 911 while pulling the baseball bat under her bed. With careful steps, she crept from her room.

The living room was dimly lit by moonlight penetrating the curtains. Her hands tightened on the wood as she struggled to penetrate the gloom when she caught a movement out of the corner of her eye, a shadow shifted in her direction. She swallowed the fear rising in her throat as she saw the figure separate from the surrounding shadows, hobbling toward her with quick but uneven steps, clawed hands outstretched.

"Please..." it hissed at her. "You are mine. Please."

"Paulette! Open up. It's Uncle Paul. You're in danger!" The hammering increased in volume.

Paulette raised the bat as the shadowy figure moved forward, now lit to reveal the horrifying ruined face with its mouth open in a silent scream. It was her face. Black and blue, cut and broken.

Paulette swung the bat; the wood connected solidly, sending the monster to the ground. She moved around the creature as it roused itself, pursuing her with a pathetic throaty hissing sound. Paulette reached the door and looked through the peephole to see her uncle standing there, healthy.

"Let me in! She's going to kill you! Let me in!!"

Paulette looked back to see the monster shuffling toward her. She gripped the bat again but knew she couldn't stop it alone. Paulette turned the lock on the door with a trembling hand and let him in.

The door flung open, and Uncle Paul rushed in, hands outstretched toward the creature. He said to Paulette, "Wake up now. You're safe. You're safe."

\*\*\*

"Hey Paulette," a tentative voice drew her from her sightless stare out the shop window. She turned to see Damon's bespectacled face looking at her intently; his curly hair reminded her of a Goldendoodle. "We all missed you these last few days. I really missed you. I'm sorry about your uncle; he must have been remarkable." He offered her a half smile and held a bright yellow mug with a calico cat for the handle. "I made you tea."

"Unlike me," Paulette muttered bitterly as she accepted the mug and sipped. Warm comfort suffused her body. She looked up to see Damon watching her, and he glanced away.

"That's not true. You are something special." The words fell away when he watched her gaze slip past him to the window outside. "If it would help take your mind off things, want to go to the five-dollar theater? They're showing, *You've Got Mail* tonight."

Damon waited anxiously, but she showed no sign of having heard him. "OK, hey. Sorry to bother you, but I just wanted to check in on you. We are all worried- even the cats." With his parting words, Damon slipped away and bussed an empty table before one of the cats found the half-eaten muffin.

\*\*\*

That evening, she found herself drawn to the video again. There had to be more to this than writing down everything she hated about herself, which, admittedly, was everything.

She ate a nut from the tin as the television buzzed and the VHS came to life. The image jumped momentarily before it resumed where it was last paused. The words "Open Yourself to Change" were superimposed over the set, with Dr Temeril's face framed in the O.

"Welcome back," came the soothing voice of the doctor. "In phase 2, we open ourselves up to change. If you aren't open to change, things will always be the same- lonely, sad, and unfulfilling. Do you remember?"

[28]

Paulette nodded. "I'm an unlovable failure that no one will miss," she replied bitterly. "I'm just a fat waste of flesh with a pathetic cat cafe and no future. God, I'm such a waste."

"That's right," the doctor said encouragingly. "I know it's hard, but you're doing great. In no time, you'll be a completely new you." The video continued: "Now is the time. I reject who I am. I reject my failed self. I kill that person and open myself to begin again as someone new, someone better."

With a tired voice, Paulette repeated the words.

Phase 3 - Clean Out the Old You

A mewling sound woke her, a pathetic whimper from the living room. Paulette frowned, not recalling bringing any cats home from the cafe; she grabbed her bat and padded softly to her bedroom door, peering into the gloom to see two figures standing near her couch.

Paulette flicked the switch by her door, and twin carnival glass lamps bloomed, spraying the walls with pastel light. The horrifying shadow creature cowered near the couch while a vaguely familiar man stood by her, holding a knife.

"Ah, she's up!" The voice was Dr. Temeril's. "Just in time for work to be done." He moved toward her, offering the knife handle first. "I caught it skulking around. Terrifying looking, isn't it? All of your weaknesses in one spot." His tone twisted cruelly as he said, "It's pathetic. Look at it."

Paulette did as the doctor told her, setting the bat against the side table and stepping around for a better look.

Frizzy brown hair was matted to its skull by dark fluids, the flesh of its face pale under the bruises and cuts. Its red-rimmed eyes were mud brown under brows that always tried to merge into one. The mouth was open as if to scream or sob, revealing rows of broken teeth. The clothes looked like a mockery of the nicest outfit she could afford, the one she wore on the opening day of Cozy Cats. Except these were torn and stained like she'd fallen in the trash. A pin glinted in the light, something Damon had gotten her for the store's third anniversary; it said, "Someone loves a crazy cat lady."

Something about the sight of the pin broke her focus until Dr. Temeril stepped into her line of sight. "To truly be open to change, you must destroy what holds you back." The black handle of the knife seemed to eat the lamplight as it lay in his hand.

Paulette grasped the cold handle, taking the knife. Dr. Temeril moved aside, and she was shocked to see the creature had moved closer, its curled fingers reaching out to her.

"Please... don't do this. I don't want to be gone. Please..." Its voice was soft, the words shallow, like someone gasping for breath.

"See?" Dr. Temeril said, moving his face so it was next to her. "Fear is tenacious. It's a parasite. It can't live without you, but you can live without your weaknesses. Don't you want to be your best? To really live?"

Paulette's eyes stung with tears as she nodded.

"Good girl, then. Let's do it." The doctor pulled away and watched.

Paulette forced herself forward, step by step, gripping the knife handle so tightly it hurt. Her arm was tense as she raised it. The creature recoiled, raising an arm to try to block. Paulette was shocked to see the arm covered in defensive scars. She looked back to Temeril. "Why does she look like that?"

Dr. Temeril leaned against the wall and took a drag from a cigarette she hadn't noticed him holding. "You've failed so many times at this, but have we given up on you? No! Now is your chance to escape your life." He paused, flicking ashes on her lamp. "Or were you happy having this thing in charge?"

She almost protested at the cigarette and ash on her favorite lamp but stopped. Who cares, she thought, it's all pointless.

The creature began to beg again when Paulette let out a throat-ripping shriek, "Fuck you!" With all her strength, Paulette reversed her grip on the knife to overhand and stabbed the wretch in its open mouth.

The blade plunged into its throat and lodged there; choking sounds came as blood bubbled up with its ragged breaths. It looked at Paulette as though she'd betrayed it before the light left its eyes.

"Gorgeous!!" Temeril cried. "Right in the fucking throat! Much better than the pathetic show your uncle put on." The cigarette flared like a tiny hell star as he finished it. With shuddering breath, like he'd just had an orgasm, he said, "Let's drag this thing out of here."

# Phase 4 - Reformat Your Mind

The following morning, Paulette realized that she needed to cut away her current life like the tumor it was. It started with a call to her uncle's lawyer asking for help finding a buyer for the space and another call to Damon to meet her at the store.

"But I don't understand, Paulette. Why are you closing the shop?" The anguish in Damon's voice was unmistakable. "The community loves it! We... we built something special here—you and me. You can't just give up on us! Please."

Paulette was surprised by the intensity of Damon's emotions and shook her head. "It's a barely successful store whose saving grace is that we have cats, " she said. As she reached into her pocket for the store keys, something caught on them - the pin he had given her.

"Barely successful?" he shouted as he pulled his phone out of his pocket. Damon tapped and swiped quickly before turning the phone to face her. "This is the last report from the accountant. We've been profitable for the past year, and that's with rising costs. We talked about expanding into the next space because we kept running out of room. Does that sound like barely successful?"

She shook her head, unable to meet his eyes. "It's not worth it. It's just not enough."

Damon slowed his breathing and closed his eyes. "What's enough, Paulette? Do you even know?"

Paulette bit her lip. She was close to finding her purpose and happiness, but Damon's pain tore at her. She buried her emotions and hardened her voice. "I want you to run an adoption event through this week. All cats must go. It should be easy. All stock is half off. Sam's Thrift truck will pick up anything not sold by Friday. Got it?"

Something flashed across his face and died before it reached his mouth. He nodded mutely, not meeting her eyes.

She set the keys on the counter with the pin. "You can have this back. Find someone deserving to give it to."

When he didn't reply or move, she sighed and turned to leave the store. Just as she got to the door, she heard him raise his emotion-laden voice, "Fuck you, Paulette! You'll never be happy because you don't know how to accept joy; nothing will ever be enough." As she turned to look at him, something flew past her face and hit the wall before clattering to the floor. The pin lay there as he said, "And I already had."

\* \* \*

"Welcome to the final phase. I'm so excited for you to achieve your destiny!" Dr. Temeril sat on the edge of his seat, a cigarette pinched in the right side of his mouth. "And good news. It's the easiest one! You've done all the hard work. Are you ready?"

Paulette nodded unselfconsciously and briefly thought about how good a cigarette sounded. "Oh, I'm ready!"

"Repeat after me. Ego sum vas inane." His voice became heavy as though he were chanting a spell.

Why the fuck not, she thought with a sense of fatalism. Why the fuck not? "Ego sum vas inane."

"Hoc vas tuum est."

"Hoc vas tuum est." A sense of giddy confidence filled her, skin tingling.

"Oblitus sum." He cried out triumphantly.

"Oblitus sum." The sense of tingling filled her whole body; Paulette felt like she was exploding and dying all at once as her consciousness slipped away.

\* \* \*

The following afternoon, Paulette went to the lawyer's office to sign the agreement to let them handle the details of the shop sale and, with a new purpose in hand, claimed her wealth.

"I'm so honored to have worked with your uncle." The lawyer said obsequiously to Paulette as he handed her a folder containing the papers showing the transfer of control of all assets to her.

Paulette smiled faintly and said, "Of course, I'm sure it was his pleasure. And thank you for all your help. Is the car waiting for me?"

The lawyer nodded eagerly and motioned to his assistant, who opened the door for her. "It's outside, waiting to take you to the airport."

Paulette turned to walk out the door, paying the lawyer and his staff no more mind. She fished a cigarette from the pack her uncle left her and pinched it on the right side of her mouth as she lit it; the cigarette flared to life as she inhaled like a drowning person tasting air again.

The driver opened the door for her, and she climbed inside. Once she was seated comfortably, he pulled away from the curb, and she opened the window to let the smoke out.

"Where are you flying to?" The driver asked in the bored but polite tone of someone making conversation.

Paulette took another long drag off the cigarette, savoring the smoke's flavor and feel. "London," She replied, and then quietly, to herself, she said, "It's been almost a century since I was there, and I have old affairs to settle."

## THE PIPE DREAM
### BY BRIAN GATTI

I waited for Dr. Pendleton in one of the many uncomfortable wooden chairs in the foyer. I had a glass of champagne bubbling on the table beside me. I seethed on the ornate, uncomfortable chair as frustration brewed within me. As a grown man, I should be free to live as I wish. Yet, as the eldest, I was the heir to my family's wealth and my mother's unrelenting expectations.

One aspect of me would love nothing more than to fail their test and let them make my brother the heir. But a stronger part raged against this thought. I am the firstborn! I've dealt with their picking, berating, and haranguing my whole life. I deserve it. Not perfect Marlon. He can live in a slum for all I care. That is where I know I'll end up if he inherits it all.

And so, I struck a deal with them. I would accept a radical new treatment from Dr. Julius Pendleton that would supposedly cure my love of opium. In exchange? I keep my position as primary heir, I get a thousand pounds, and my parents get some sort of compensation.

All in exchange for my beloved opium.

I had no plan to keep my promise, of course. Once my parents were dead, I could live as I wished. God willing, the money I've paid Gilcrest, and his merry band of thugs will help my parents to their great reward.

I was reaching for the neglected glass of champagne when the door opened from the library. It admitted a tall, slender woman with pale skin in a nurse's uniform. "Mr. Huston, are you ready?"

I opened my mouth to speak but found myself arrested by her appearance. She was not beautiful. Her green-stained lips curved in an expression that looked like a mockery of a smile. Her face was porcelain smooth but, in a literal way, looked more like a doll than a human being.

It was disconcerting as I drank in her imperfect perfection and felt a familiar stir in my pants. Perhaps I could arrange an after-visit.

If she knew what was happening in my mind, she gave no sign. Except maybe for a tightening at the corners of her eyes as though in restrained amusement.

I averted my gaze and approached the library door. Affixed to the inside of the door was a large, 8-pointed star with brass letters ADF above it.

I walked into the library behind the nurse. Inside waited Dr. Pendleton. He cut a tall, slim silhouette against the light of the fire. The room was a study made of burnished wood and green lead glass, giving the room an inviting atmosphere. Over the fireplace was an unusual family crest. It was of an octopus coiled around a two-masted merchant ship holding objects aloft in its tentacles. Written underneath was the phrase, 'Devorabit Omnia' below the image.

Dr. Pendleton smiled thinly, "Welcome, Alex, to my humble office." He pointed to one of six white calfskin leather chairs. Each of them was large and overstuffed to the point of absurdity.

I glanced at them and then settled into the one he directed me to, closest to the fire. It had been chilly outside, and this was most welcoming.

I sat in the generously padded chair. It embraced me like fat Aunt Margaret, uncomfortably warm and with too many soft bulges. Dr. Pendleton's reedy voice directed me, "Please take a moment to settle. The chair may initially be overwhelming, but it's here to give you comfort and safety."

I sank into it as I sat there. Each movement caused me to settle deeper into its plushness. It was like cozy quicksand but without the drowning death at the end.

"Comfortable?"

I nodded, my mouth suddenly dry.

"Wonderful. We are participating in a pharmacological study with people who currently smoke opium. During this study, you'll be asked to smoke a modified blend of opium. It is designed to eliminate any further desire for it. Are you still willing?"

*Only in the way a hostage is a willing participant in a kidnapping,* I thought as bitter emotions bubbled inside. But I kept this to myself as I nodded again, licking my lips. "Can I have some water?"

Dr. Pendleton's bland smile creased briefly at my interruption. However, he motioned to the woman dressed as a nurse, who left without speaking.

"When was the last time you used opium?"

The nurse returned and handed me a green-tinted crystal goblet filled with water. I swallowed eagerly before saying, "Ahh, well, as per your instructions, I haven't in the past week." I paused as I fought the sense of nausea that I'd been battling since I began abstaining. "It's been a very hard week."

Dr. Pendleton took the goblet from me and handed it to the nurse. "Well, we are very grateful for your strict adherence to the program. It will help ensure the success of the treatment. The process is very precise."

He sat on the table's edge, so we were eye to eye. "Now, you should be aware that previous participants have reported feelings of euphoria and vivid visions. Most importantly, they discovered a complete elimination of the desire to smoke in the future. The nurse and I will monitor your entire session to ensure your safety. Do you understand?"

"Yes," I croaked out, my throat dry again. "And... the compensation..." between the chair and the fire, I was becoming drowsy and warm. I suddenly wanted this over.

The doctor cut me off. "£1,000 for you when the treatment is complete, as promised." He removed an envelope filled with cash and set it on the table beside me. As he did this, the nurse brought the opium pipe and set it before me. It was unusual, maybe crafted from jade. It glittered green but with a blood-red tint in the firelight. The top opened as she pressed the mixture to the saddle.

I refrained from licking my lips as the heady scent of quality opium hit me. My mouth watered in anticipation. "I'm ready."

Dr. Pendleton smiled again and touched a burning twig to the lamp on the pipe, igniting it. I took several experimental puffs to draw the air through and aid the process. A strong hit of the smoke came... and I was gone.

For me, opium isn't only about the high. It's the whole experience. There's the smell of it before it's burnt. I imagine it is similar to the smell of primeval forests, so rich. This had that scent, but it was tainted with the foul, eggy stink of sulfur.

Usually, the smoke is sweet yet coy. Yet, whatever was in the added medicine made it sharp and strident, like being scolded.

When the smoke hit my lungs, it was like being embraced by thick, sun-soaked mud. Warm and inescapable, pulling my unresisting mind under.

Peace found me, and I was no longer afraid. I was no longer myself. I had transformed into a glorious non-being, unburdened by pain. There were no expectations of the sour sadness that came with the knowledge I'd never be enough for my parents.

In my beautiful pipe dream, none of that mattered. I could simply be. The agonizing thoughts leaked away from my mind like poison drawn from a wound. I succumbed to the opium's power, drifting lower into the dream space, my one true happy place.

I lived in a house by the beach. The sand was warm under my feet. Great basalt cliffs encircled the beach with endless black stone arms. It was a comforting embrace. I fished in the bay in my boat enjoying a simple life. Fishing brings dangers, but I know them.

I looked over the boat's edge. The green water flexed with gentle waves, and silvery fish darted below. An octopus lazily floated on the waves as fish struggled in its tentacles. I watched with delight and inspired by the eight-armed creature's languid movement in the water. I dove in. The cool water embraced me, soaking me through my clothing as I floated on my back. It was as though, instead of staring up, I gazed down at the cloudless blue sky suspended above it by gravity.

My body dipped and rose. I drifted on the surface of consciousness in the bay of controlled reality. A lull came over me as I was gently carried toward the mouth of the bay.

The waves carried me from my boat, and I was not afraid. I wondered, what's past the break? I didn't move my limbs to swim, but thinking about the mouth of the bay drew me closer to the ocean. Closer to its dangers, and delights. My boat was barely a dot in the great beyond now, occasionally obscured by a wave. I was still calm.

Somehow the water was looser, as though its elements were too far apart. I struggled to stay buoyant. The water was no longer tangible enough to hold me up.

The water grew colder as some clouds covered the sun. The waves remained gentle and became foamy. Is it evaporating beneath me? I dipped below the waves into the dark water. The foam was lit by the sun-like milky stars. I rose again, took a deep breath, and tasted the troubling and unfamiliar flavor of the sulphuric water.

I could no longer stay above the surface. The greenish water tinted the world, giving the sun and sky the hue of an alien world. I held my breath as the light from above faded. Silvery bubbles floated past my descending body. Their delicacy tickled my skin and left it tingling.

The water's weight pushed me down. The tingling sensation grew worse as the bubbles raced past me to the surface, as though they gloried in their freedom. The cold and dark were unwelcome additions to my drugged oblivion. I reached helplessly upwards, grasping at the airy water.

My chest screamed for me to breathe. An animal panic filled me! I wanted so much to live, to fight against the merciless indifference of the ocean. I hated my real life so, buried in soul-deep sadness. Only opium helped me escape. I knew I was willing to trade my life for this moment of wonder and terror, but my animal self cried out to live. It would fight anything for one more breath. Something I knew I should not do.

Pearls of air slid between my lips, rocketing upwards as my chest ached. The tingling sensation turned to burning. I was cold and on fire, reaching the end of my sanity as I felt the darkness close in at the edges of my vision.

At last, my final breath erupted from my mouth with the violence of a submarine at crush depth. I was at crush depth. My body gently landed on the slime-covered stones at the bottom, and I inhaled. I had no choice; the animal mind won and didn't know we were dead.

\* \* \*

Dr. Pendleton watched Alex's body sag in the chair. Only his head remained visible before disappearing into the creature's soft, leathery flesh. It was an infant Devourer. The other five babies gave up the pretense of being chairs, transformed back into their original form, and opened their mouths. Their maws were filled with glittering, green teeth. They keened in unison, a cry of celebration, and yearning. They all longed to be fed next.

The doctor affectionately stroked the creature's pale hide. He looked up at the nurse who had walked in awkwardly carrying a burlap sack. A gooey viscera seeped through and shone black on the floor in the light of the fire. She looked at the creature Alex had been fed to. Her eyes raised.

"Yes, sister," the doctor said. "She's accepted the offering. It is glorious, and we are much closer. We must complete the ritual now."

"Glory to the ADF!! Glory to the All-Devouring Flesh!" She cried out, joy suffusing her waxen features.

His chants joined hers. "Glory to the Great Feasting. Grateful to serve The Ravenous One!"

As she spoke, she reached her delicate hand into the bag. Pulling out chunks of flesh, she tossed them to the hungry babies. One was a beard-covered slice of face caught in the mouth of the closest one before being pulled in by a tentacle-like tongue.

"The Huston family has kept their bargain," Dr. Pendleton said with satisfaction. The infant Devourer seemed to shrink in on itself as it digested its meal. The doctor looked at his sister as she licked the gore from her fingers. "Prepare it to go home and begin its new life as Alex Huston."

PORTRAIT OF A KILLER                                BY T.D. BARTON

"I'll have it for you in two weeks." Thad Hawley hung up the phone, tucked it in his pocket, and walked across the room with a manilla envelope. He pulled out a photograph and attached it to the upper right-hand corner of his easel with a push pin. A confident, energetic man with dark hair graying at the temples smiled back at him.

The man stood before a wood-paneled wall that screamed posh office setting. Thomas Hawking was the CEO of Westbrook Industries. It was his secretary, Ms. Fields, whom Ed had been talking to. According to the letter that had accompanied the photo, his grateful employees had decided to commission Thad. They wanted him to create a portrait of Mr. Hawking to grace the wall behind his desk.

This was a typical assignment for Thad Hawley, an artist specializing in oil portraiture. He was an even six-foot tall with chaotic red hair that indicated his independence and lack of interest in conforming to style or custom. In other words, it screamed that he didn't give a rat's ass about his outward appearance. He was a consummate fine artist, very serious about his work.

But the portraiture and other commissioned work paid the bills. That part of his artwork was necessary if he were to continue to afford his studio here on the fourth floor of a building in the Soho district. After twenty-three years of gaining a name for himself, Thad's regular pieces were finally selling for a moderately respectable price. Yet, they did not bring in enough to support him in the style he desired. It was only by combining that income with the commissioned work that he could survive.

He had artwork hanging all over the city which he was quite proud of. Some were in private collections, and some were available in prominent galleries. Others were commissioned works such as murals. One was a marvelous depiction of the city's skyscape that adorned the ground floor of this very building.

This particular job appeared to be an easy one. It would be a simple portrait, one he could knock off in a week, maybe two tops. He had told

Ms. Fields two weeks because, over the years, he had found that sometimes, things might come up to delay a project. It was always a good idea to give yourself a little flexibility. Promise long and deliver short, he chuckled to himself. No one was ever upset if you finished a job in less time than was quoted.

With a sigh, Thad seated himself before his large easel. He then attached a blank, pre-treated canvas and began laying out the materials he would need for this project. He gathered various pencils, charcoal sticks, erasers, fixatives, and sketch paper on a table by his side. He fanned out several brushes and prepared Sansodour, a low-odor solvent, and refined linseed oil for thinning and brush cleaning. Along with these items, he set out a clean palette, and palette knife, and six palette cups for preserving mixed tints. Near the table's edge sat a large roll of paper towels and a rag, covered with multicolored splotches from previous cleanups.

Within a few minutes, he had everything he would need on the table and arranged to be handy and within reach. He adjusted his easel to collect as much natural light as possible from the large windows. Pulling the photograph of Mr. Hawking from the easel, he held it in front of his face.

Thad studied the picture intently for about twenty minutes, gathering information, mentally cataloging it for reference, and overall preparing himself to begin. Another thing he had learned when it came to portrait work: never present the subject as he or she actually looked in the reference photo. The trick was to get the basics of how the subject appears but then embellish and flatter them as much as possible without losing the features that made them recognizable. He would shave off a few pounds here or there, thinning the face, straightening out crooked teeth, maybe slimming down that nose a bit.

When he was just starting out, he had many instances where he had prepared a perfectly fine representation of a client faithfully recreating the reference photos only to have the customer unhappy with the results. To please a client, the portrait has to portray the subject as how they see themselves in their own mind rather than how they are in real life.

So, he would begin, using pencil and charcoal nibs to sketch out his subject along with the elegant background. First general shapes were laid down and then, little by little, more detail was added, and the scale was checked repeatedly. The distance between the pupils of the eyes, the length of the nose and the upper lip, the shape of the chin, cheekbones, and forehead, all these things, and dozens more were meticulously plotted out and double-checked.

Working with practiced hands and discerning eyes, Thad completed the preliminary sketch in no time. Satisfied at last with his work on the face, neck, shirt collar, and business suit of the CEO, he began laying in the color for the background. The basic hues for the wood paneling soon surrounded the penciled-in face and shoulders of Mr. Hawking.

Thad paid special attention to the lighting as he began shading in the facial features. He worked tirelessly, completely absorbed in his work. This is why Thad Hawley became an artist. Nothing in his life provided him with such happiness, such fulfillment, and peace of mind. Hours could go by in the outside world, but Thad wouldn't know it. He was happy living his life one brush stroke at a time.

He had tried his luck with romance and domestic bliss, but his artwork always took precedence over whatever was happening in his life. This was what led his wife Diane to divorce him. In Thad's world, his self-image presented him first as an artist, and secondly as an artist with a wife. A wife who, early on, sometimes interrupted him in his work and pulled him back into this mundane disaster of a life. It took only a little bit to break her of that bad habit and to train her not to interfere when he was working. And Thad was at work a lot of the time. He loved his work.

Of course, Diane accused him of loving his art more than her, and if he were to be honest with himself, he would have to admit that to be true. But any great artist is only concerned with truth as he sees it — reality as only he can present it.

Unfortunately, that's not the way the judge saw things and the divorce had cost him dearly in the way of alimony. This was another reason he had to try so hard to sell his artwork.

It was well after three o'clock before his tired eyes and aching back agreed with his rumbling stomach that it was time for lunch. Thad cleaned the brush he was currently holding and stood up. For a few moments, he gazed at the canvas and the work he had so far completed and then at last moved off into the kitchen to prepare himself something to eat.

After lunch, Thad resumed his work and continued well into the evening. At last, when the little clock on the kitchen counter emitted a "ding" he realized it was time to stop for the day. The timer was something he had set up long ago to avoid becoming so engrossed in his work as to be detrimental to his health. Thad had learned that he must put limits upon himself, or he would burn out and wind up neglecting his own care.

It was ten o'clock exactly. Thad had made sure the alarm would remind him every night at precisely this time. Usually, he was disciplined enough to stop whatever he was doing and rest. But sometimes, if he was particularly absorbed, he would irritably dismiss the alarm and keep on working. This usually occurred when he was especially inspired by an original creation and couldn't be bothered with health concerns.

Most of the time at the end of the day, he would pour himself a glass of wine, turn on some music or TV, unwind for about an hour, and then go to bed. Thad rarely bothered with dinner, finding it perfectly fine to exist on two meals a day.

Tonight, when the bell tolled, he sighed and stood to clean up. As he wiped down the area and cleaned his brushes and palettes, he examined the partially finished painting.

Smiling contentedly, he congratulated himself on the progress he had made. The basic colors for the entire piece were laid down and the eyes had been nearly finished with only a few details to be worked in. Thad always roughed in the eyes first and then moved on to the other facial features one by one. The eyes were the key to the personality. They went a long way toward capturing the soul of the subject. Every other detail could be presented perfectly but if the eyes weren't right, the entire work of art would be worthless.

The last thing he did was to cover the painting with a light cloth carefully so as not to smudge the paint.

He pushed his hands into the small of his back to stretch, poured himself a glass of wine, and flopped down on the couch. With a grin of satisfaction, he picked up the controller and clicked on the television. After about thirty minutes he found himself dozing off and decided to turn in for the evening. The screen went blank, and he walked into the bedroom, removing his clothes along the way, and dropped into bed where he was out almost immediately.

\* \* \* \*

Thad whistled a soft, lively tune as he slipped two pieces of bacon into a pan and scrambled some eggs. A single slice of buttered toast rounded out his meal along with a hot cup of coffee.

He finished his breakfast while reading the New York Times and washed up the dishes afterward. Pouring himself another cup of coffee, he walked over to the huge windows and looked out over the street below. Cars and people jammed the streets and sidewalks, and he gave a small shudder, thanking his lucky stars that he wasn't among them. These days he doesn't go out much (even your groceries can now be delivered) and when he is working on a piece, he doesn't leave the studio at all. He had pretty much all he needed right here.

Smacking his lips he took another sip of coffee and sat down before his easel. He rested the coffee on the side table, reached up, and whisked the cover from the painting. Immediately, the smile left his face. He stared wide-eyed at the portrait before him and knitted his brows.

Thad looked over at the photograph penned to his easel and ripped it away. He held it in front of his face, then moved it over beside the painting.

"What th —" he said out loud and his voice was filled with wonder. "That's — This is impossible."

The painting was just as he had left it, with basic colors filled in, and facial features depicted accurately except for one thing. The eyes were different. The shape didn't conform to the photo at all. They were closer together and squinting slightly in a menacing sort of way as though their owner intended harm of some kind.

Thomas Hawking had soft, clear eyes that reflected both knowledge and a type of kindness that anyone would hope to see in the eyes of their employer. A deep languid brown, they seemed to express trustworthiness and capability.

As Thad gawked silently at the canvas, the eyes glaring back at him were hard and cold with an evil glint and a heavy dose of malice.

And they were blue. A light, steely blue.

Thad stood up. "Somebody's been screwing around with my work!" he shouted. He looked around the studio and then moved rapidly through the flat, checking and securing every room and door. There was no one there but him.

He sat back down and stared at the canvas for a long time. Finally, he pulled off a paper towel and soaked it in a solvent. Then, oh so gently, he dabbed at the paint that depicted the eyes, trying to remove the top layer to see if the original paint was there, underneath, where he had put it yesterday. But there was nothing beneath except white canvas. Not even the pencil sketches remained.

"That's NOT what I painted!" Thad screamed in rage. Thomas Hawking stared back at him with what was left of his new eyes and said nothing.

The bewildered artist sat before his easel staring at the work for a full hour and nothing came out of his mouth save for once when he emitted a strangled HUH!

At last, he stiffly reached over and picked up his pallet, preparing it with various colors shades, and hues. When this was done, he took up his brushes and began restoring the soft brown eyes of Mr. Hawking to their original luster.

When the kitchen timer dinged, Thad stood immediately and gazed at the work in progress. Now he had faithfully completed the nose and mouth as well as having restored the kind eyes of the CEO. Again, he covered the canvas and poured a glass of wine. This time, however, he didn't turn on the TV. Rather, he sat quietly listening to the sounds of the city outside his walls, quickly drank the wine, and went to bed.

\* \* \* \*

Sleep hadn't come easily that night, but eventually, he nodded off. In the morning, he resisted the urge to immediately remove the cover and look at the painting. He prepared his breakfast as usual, sat at the small kitchen table, and stared at the covered work while he ate, stared while drinking his coffee, and stared as he washed up. At last, second cup in hand, he sat at his stool, and, with trembling fingers, he ripped away the cover, screamed, and jumped to his feet.

Just as he had feared, the face of Mr. Hawking was no longer there. Instead, there was a lewd, twisted scowling man with harsh features and a murderous look in his eye. Nothing of the detailed work he had done to depict the beloved CEO remained. Another evil-looking face had replaced it and it seemed to be directing its baleful leering glare, particularly at Thad. Hatred seethed from those angry eyes and that tortured mouth. It was as though the man on the canvas considered himself wronged in some way and, although Thad had never before laid eyes on him, he blamed the artist for some perceived injury.

"Who are you?" Thad howled. "What do you want from me?"

Thad got up and checked the locks on the front door and all the windows. There was definitely no way anyone could be entering his loft and altering his painting. Besides, he had to admit that the changes to his canvas appeared to be in his style. This brutal new face, whoever it was, was painted just as he would have done. Was it possible he was walking in his sleep? Was this some sort of somnambulistic joke on himself?

If that were true, there would be evidence of his efforts showing on his worktable. Things would have been moved around, brushes used in different order, palettes prepared with different colors and hues.

But that was not the case, everything was exactly as he had left it last evening. Nothing had been touched.

He couldn't understand how or why this was happening. Was it some kind of supernatural warning from beyond the grave? Was some unearthly messenger trying to tell him something? As he stared at the strange face in the painting, a feeling of dread came over him. It was a sense of foreboding, and he shuddered, trying not to think of it.

The studio remained silent, and, after a while, Thad picked up his brushes and began again.

\* \* \* \*

Thad Hawley worked harder on this piece than he had ever worked in his life. Frantically, he painted over the loathsome face that glared angrily up at him from the canvas and replaced it with the calm, placid visage of CEO Thomas Hawking one more time. He added layer upon layer working feverishly to finish the painting. The desperate artist wanted nothing more than to be finished with it and have it out of his life.

When the bell dinged, he ignored it and worked on, striving to see it through. The hours flew by as Thad, completely absorbed in what he was doing, painted with zeal combined with precision. He worked all night and past the break of the next morning.

There had been no glass of wine, no morning breakfast of eggs and bacon, nothing but the painting existed. At this moment, it was the most important thing in the artist's life.

At last, it was finished.

Thad stood up and gazed uncertainly upon it. He studied it, looking for flaws. He held up the photo of Thomas Hawking and compared it with his work. Reluctantly, he had to admit it was very good. The highlights glinted brilliantly, and the shadows cast the perfect amount of contrast. The face fairly glowed with personality. Slowly it dawned on him that it was the best work he had ever accomplished, commissioned or otherwise. It was ... his masterpiece! His heart hammered in his chest as he stood back and appreciated it.

He looked at the clock. It was midmorning. Ten o'clock to be precise. With a little laugh, he pulled out his phone and dialed a number.

It was answered on the third ring. "Ms. Fields?" he said. "Ms. Fields, this is Thad Hawley." (pause) "Oh yes, I'm fine, thank you. Ms. Fields, I'm calling you to let you know that the portrait you requested has been completed (pause) Yes, that's right I did say two weeks but, uh, well, I had such a great time working on such a handsome and charismatic man as Mr. Hawking that I'm happy to say that I finished way ahead of schedule."

Promise long and deliver short he thought and nearly laughed out loud.

"Yes, that's right. Now, Ms. Fields, I'm going to be going out of town unexpectedly and I would really, really appreciate it if you could pick up the painting immediately (pause) Yes, now you'll have to give it time to dry, but I will wrap it to protect it until you can have it framed ... no really, I can't wait." (He couldn't stop his voice from rising an octave) "I have to have it out of here! (pause) Today? Oh, that would be wonderful. No, I'll bill your company later — when I get back. (pause) Oh, thank you very much. Goodbye."

Thad walked over and studied the magnificent painting one more time then reluctantly covered it and, even though it was early, he went for the wine. In the kitchen, he reconsidered and moved instead to the liquor cabinet. He'd decided a glass of bourbon would go farther toward soothing his nerves.

He was on his third glass when a loud knock came from the door. Ms. Fields already? he asked himself. Rising from the couch he passed the covered painting and approached the door. "Who's there?" he called.

"Grocery delivery!" came a muffled voice.

Thad didn't remember ordering groceries but, in his woozy state of compromised sobriety, he shook it off. He opened the door and screamed in shock.

Standing in the doorway, steely blue eyes blazing was the scowling figure that had kept appearing in his paintings. The one he could not be rid of. It was the same crooked, scowling mouth, the same stubbled chin, and short gray prison haircut. The man stood for a moment and glared at him menacingly. Then he pushed the artist back into the room, slamming the door closed behind them.

Thad fell backward on the floor and whined, looking up at the glowering man. "Who are you? What do you want?" The furious man spat and said, "I know you don't remember me, but I think you'll remember my wife." He held a wrinkled photograph in one trembling hand. (In the other he clutched a long, wicked-looking knife.)

He waved the picture in front of Thad's eyes. "Do ya?" he shouted hoarsely.

Thad blinked and tried to focus on the picture. "N - no," he sputtered.

"Look again!" the man shouted and shoved the photo in Thad's face.

"All her life my Carla had wanted to be in pictures," he said. "It's all she ever dreamed of. And she'd have made it too if it wasn't for you. Mister big shot artist! Mister portrait painter!"

"One year, for our anniversary I decided to surprise her with an authentic oil portrait. I didn't think anybody could capture her beauty but you ... you assured me you were the man for the job. So, I paid you the money and you brought her in and had her pose nude to do a portrait. And how'd it come out? Well, let's just say not too good." He shoved another picture in Thad's face.

Thad was staring wide-eyed at the photograph as it danced wildly before his eyes. His unkempt hair drooped down over his sweat-covered forehead and partially blocked his vision. But still, he could see well enough to begin to recognize the painting. It was all coming back to him now. He remembered the assignment and the model. Was she the one who had been trying to warn him? Had it been the ghost of the now-dead Carla reaching out from beyond? She knew the man's temper, knew what he was capable of...

"Look, that was when I was first starting out. I didn't have much experience yet. I ---" his head drooped. "I'll admit it wasn't my best work."

"No, it sure wasn't," the man growled.

"I gave her your money back when you said you didn't like it..." Thad offered.

The man kicked Thad squarely in the face and his head flew back striking the floor hard.

"That's not the point" the intruder snarled. "The thing is when Carla saw her picture, and how she thought she must really look, it broke her. She lost her confidence. All she wanted to do was mope around the house. I tried to tell her how beautiful she was, but she just wouldn't take it from me. Said I was prejudiced. That I had to say that because I was her husband. She gave up on her dreams altogether."

"I got in trouble and wound up going to prison for a short stretch. Carla said she would wait for me. When I got out, I found out she had taken to drinking and was in really bad shape. She definitely wasn't the beauty she had been that's for sure. Looked more like she did in your stupid painting. But I loved her anyway."

As Thad lay on the floor with his head throbbing, the man's eyes filled with tears. "Then, a couple weeks ago she threw herself off the Brooklyn Bridge. She just couldn't live with the pain anymore."

He glared down at Thad and gripped the knife harder in his hand. "You did that to my Carla. You killed her dreams with your filthy paint and brushes. It only took me a little while to find you and now here I am." He brandished the knife in a sinister way, hate and fury filled his eyes.

"That painting wasn't meant to be a realistic representation," Thad whined. He coiled his fingers in his dark red hair and held his head. Blood trickled out from between them. "It was meant to show the woman inside and the turmoil she was going through. Her unfulfilled dreams... the yearning soul within ... the inner beauty."

"Liar!" screamed the man.

He plunged the knife into Thad's chest several times, then stood over him looking down at the dying body and panting while Thad's life drained away. The blood was brighter than alizarin crimson as it pooled on the artist's floor. After a time, the killer's breathing returned to normal, and he walked slowly around the room. He sat for a little while on Thad's couch, finished his bourbon, and then left, closing the door behind him.

\* \* \* \*

Detective Alex Henderson sat at Thad's kitchen table while Ms. Fields nursed a cup of coffee across from him. She was a slim woman in her mid-thirties wearing a dark blue modest business suit and white ruffled shirt. She wore little makeup, a light blush rose-hued lipstick, and eyeliner, which was now smeared and nearly removed by her tears. Her wire-rimmed glasses were pushed up on her forehead.

"The door was closed, but after I knocked, I found it wasn't locked and I came on in. That's when I found him," she said.

The police had been there for some time now and it seemed to her they kept asking the same questions over and over.

"As I said, my company had commissioned Mr. Hawley to do a painting of our CEO, and he called me to say I could come pick it up." She sniffled a little bit and dabbed her nose with a tissue but by now most of the shock was wearing off and she seemed calm.

Henderson stood and approached the easel in the middle of the room. He reached up and pulled the protective cover from the painting. "Is this him?" he asked. He indicated the painting.

Ms. Fields scrunched up her face. "Why, no. That's not Mr. Hawking. I don't know who that is."

"I do," came the voice of Seargent Klausen. He walked over to stand in front of the painting. "That's Emmet Hersh. I'd know him anywhere. Busted him a few years back on a robbery charge. Did some time. Might be out now though."

Henderson gazed at the picture and then the photo of Mr. Hawking pinned to the easel. He wasn't sure what to make of it, but there might be a lead of some kind there.

"Check and see if this guy Hersh is around, will ya? And if he is, bring him in, and let's talk to him."

"You got it," Klausen said. He looked again at the painting. "Say, that's the spitting image of Hersh. One helluva portrait I gotta say. That guy Hawley must've been some kinda painter."

*LATE NIGHT DINNER GUESTS    BY DEREK BARTON*


Chuck Broward loaded the last bag of garden fertilizer into the bed of his white pickup truck. He then placed a fifteen-foot roll of hexagonal chicken wire on the passenger seat. He glanced at his watch and sees that it is 9:08 PM.

It was a humid, muggy evening and far too late for him to be starting this errand. It was way too late for a man of sixty-two years of age to be out shopping. But he had made a promise to Emmaline, his lovely granddaughter. Last Spring, he said they would build a garden together in the backyard before Fall came to Dermott.

Earlier, on their weekly phone call, she had admonished him. "It's already mid-August! Are we going to have to buy snow shovels before we start?" Her voice rose in pitch whenever she complained. It was cute. And this little eight-year-old knew the exact buttons to push.

So...this was the weekend. He would make good on his word on Sunday.

He wiped at his sweaty brow and cursed his aching hips. "God! Don't let me have a heart attack in the middle of setting this up."

He turned the key and started the old Chevy. Traffic on the surface streets was docile but when he merged onto the I-18 freeway, it was busy. Most were young people heading out for a night of dancing and drinking, he supposed. His days of carousing were long ago, and his wife Marcy had also long since passed.

He smiled to himself at the sudden memory of her. Not a day had gone by that he hadn't thought of her and missed her laughter. He was good at making her giggle or even cackle like an old-timey witch. It was such an endearing trait of hers. Was...

He shook his head to clear away the emotions building inside, leaned over, and fished around inside his glove compartment for his pack of cigs. His twenty-eight-year-old doctor had demanded he quit. Easy for him to say, but this dirty habit had been going on longer than that little pissant had been alive!

A rusty van coated in splotchy flat black paint roared by him and cut across his lane nearly clipping Chuck's front end. It careened into the fast lane and then tailgated a semi-tractor-trailer.

"You idiot! Learn to drive before you kill someone!" He screamed. Nothing was more evident to him that the country was going to Hell than the way young people drove nowadays. Always in a frenzied rush, careless, and completely unaware of the other drivers on the road.

His sudden temper boiled. He rolled down his window and stuck out his arm to flip the van's driver off.

The van's brake lights flashed for a second. As if the vehicle itself had taken notice of Chuck's derisive slight.

Traffic began to slow further as luck would have it due to a minor fender-bender somewhere ahead. Chuck was still in the slow lane but only two cars were behind the van. The ugly van's passenger window was up and tinted very black. He could identify the make now. It was a late model GMC Savana with balding tires, sagging shocks on the back driver side with two cracked and painted-over rear windows.

Somehow Chuck felt eyes crawling all over him as if he was being studied as well. "Oh yeah?" he yelled. "That's right! You can go fuck yourself if you won't drive right!" He flipped them off again.

There was no reply, and the lanes restarted their progress. Yet when the traffic opened up, the van crept along and stayed parallel with his pickup.

A mile passed then two... The pair of vehicles remained even in the lanes.

*You don't frighten me, pal,* Chuck thought. He glanced subconsciously at the passenger seat. There, hidden underneath, was a small, silver aluminum baseball bat. From his experience as an outside salesman for an office furniture company, he always carried some form of protection. You never knew who you might encounter. He shied away from guns as it required a lot of paperwork and government bullshit regulation. Yet a leather sap, blackjack stick, or a bat was easy and still as effective.

Ahead he spotted the 209A exit ramp, his stop. He veered away. The van slowed then cut back to follow behind him. One of the van's headlights was oddly dimmed, angled to the side. It reminded him of Chester Conklin, a kid in his childhood neighborhood who had a crooked smile and a lazy eye. Talking with Chester was always awkward and off-putting. His lazy eye gave you the impression he wasn't listening, and he was more interested in something else behind you. This GMC van was kind of the same. It was watching you, but it was also angling to see what else was out there to the side. *Hunting?...*

The exit ramp circled back on itself and then marched up to a red stop light at a busy four-lane street called Adams Avenue.

Chuck waited on edge, the traffic light taking infinitely long. In his rear-view mirror, he watched the van pull up behind him. All he could see were a pair of white hands gripping a steering wheel. The interior was pitch black and hid the driver's features.

"What's your play here?" he asked aloud. The audacity of the driver was fanning the fires of his anger. "Didn't like me cussing at ya? Well, go sit down with the other bitches waiting to see if I give a shit!"

The light turned green, but Chuck paused and sat at the stop. The van revved its engine in irritation but didn't honk the horn. Finally, he accelerated and made a right turn down the street. The GMC followed. He sighed out loud, feeling put out. He wasn't looking for a confrontation. He was only expressing his own irritation at how the other driver was driving. Yet now he couldn't avoid the guy, nor could he even proceed home.

As he approached another traffic light, he decided to go left versus right. The van roared forward and blasted ahead in a sudden burst of speed. It then pitched to the left, cutting off Chuck again in the same manner he had on the freeway. This time a small, brown paper sack was vaulted out from the passenger's window. When it hit Chuck's windshield, a thin orange liquid splashed and coated the glass.

Immediately Chuck had to brake and park. He cursed vehemently as he switched on the wipers. A broad, half-circle smear followed the wipers. It was a cheap paint of some kind!

He stepped out from the truck and dug around in the collected trash inside the truck bed. He found a pair of red rags. "You son-of-a-bitch! I'm going to call the cops. No screw that! If I see you again, I'm going to go to third base on your head with my bat!" His words and rage flowed profusely from his mouth. "You went too far. Now I have the right to bash your freaking head in! Goddamn—," his ranting faded away, and his attempts to mop at the paint stopped. The black, intimidating van sat idle along the street facing him. Watching and waiting... *Hunting?*

"YOU ARE GONNA PAY!" Chuck screamed as he bolted back into the truck. He slammed his foot on the pedal and his Chevy jumped forward as it gunned toward the van. The truck's door swung closed with a bang.

He hadn't even shut it before taking off. He only saw red. His fury controlled his actions.

The black van raced off going past Chuck who had to do an awkward, ugly U-turn in the middle of the street. Now with the orange paint spread all over. It gave him only a tiny circle of window to see through where his rag had cleaned off some of the coating. He didn't care. He sped up until he was nearly crashing into the other vehicle's back bumper. There was an Ohio license plate swinging back and forth as it was held on by one bolt. He didn't bother with memorizing the numbers. This guy was not getting away from him now.

Together the pair of vehicles raced at dangerous speeds through a residential neighborhood. Chuck was panting, sweat dripping down his temples. However, he was grinning. A big, toothy smile that promised pain and punishment.

The van abruptly took a hard right that he couldn't anticipate or copy. His truck went straight and plowed into a chain link fence and exploded through someone's mailbox. Letters, advertisements, and junk newspapers went everywhere and somersaulted in the air. He had the presence of mind now to stop and catch his breath. If that had been a car or a house, he would have careened right through them. Could have even died or killed someone in the process.

"Aw shit," he moaned. "What the hell am I doing?"

At that moment bright lights lit up his truck's interior. Two headlights on full bright, one lamp still skewed to the left, came straight on. *Oh god! He's going to ram me!* Chuck screamed inside.

Again, with supernatural agility, the van twisted to the side narrowly missing the Chevy. A soda bottle arched high into the air. It came again from the passenger side window. The plastic container hit and lodged in the hood between the wiper blades spilling its contents. A putrid, acidic odor of urine filled Chuck's nose. It burned as if the bottle was poured directly into his nostrils.

HE PISSED ON YOU! His brain screamed in outrage, stunned again by the audacity of this bastard. HE JUST PISSED ON YOU! HE PISSED ALL OVER YOUR TRUCK AND YOU ARE JUST TAKING IT! PISSED ON--

Chuck saw the man at the same time he shot his arm inside the driver-side window. He thrust a dirty, white t-shirt against Chuck's face. It reeked of strong chemicals. The other driver was young, in his late twenties, and had long, choppy black hair that obscured his eyes.

His vision blurred. He didn't get a chance to mutter even a word before plummeting into nothingness.

Hours later maybe, it could've been days. Chuck didn't know, but he finally woke up. The night was still very dark and without wind. Stars peeked down at him from behind wisps of clouds as if curious as to what he was doing. His whole body ached and protested at the strain it was under. His head was held back by layers of duct tape, exposing his neck. His arms were tied together behind a tall telephone pole with a lamp that towered over him. A long strand of Christmas lights was wound around his chest and down his legs. Wood splinters of the pole poked into his back through the thin material of his gray and blue t-shirt.

Standing on the edge of light and smoking a cigarette was the young man who had attacked him. He wore faded blue jeans, a dingy green shirt, and had a cheap black leather jacket on. The kid faced away and hadn't noticed Chuck was awake yet.

In his limited field of vision, he saw an old dark barn. The black GMC Savana was parked inside. A dozen or so yards behind it, he saw his Chevy Tahoe abandoned with other neglected cars and trucks in an overgrown field. Beyond the small parking lot of vehicles were mounds of trash. They encircled the area. The smell of rot and discarded refuse hung heavy in the air like pollution. Chuck guessed it was a local junkyard.

"Mister?" Chuck mumbled. His throat and his lips were sandpaper dry. "Mister? I'm--I'm sorry."

The lanky young man turned slowly around. His face was pasty white, tattoos blanketed his neck, and silver skull earrings dangled from wide, gauged earlobes. "What's that?" he asked.

"I said, I am sorry. So very sorry. Can we forget all this happened?" Chuck pleaded. Moisture gathered at the corners of his eyes. He had never had this type of intense experience. Never been so afraid of what could happen next.

"Sorry? For what? I don't understand." He seemed genuinely confused.

A raspy, high-pitched voice called out. "Is he awake? Is he awake now?" The words were frantic and rushed, tumbling over each other in their urgency.

"Please, man. Let me go. I have a family. I...I have a beautiful granddaughter I very much want to see again. Please!"

The youth laughed. "We all have family. All have someone we need. I have a sister, man." A shadow seemed to pass over his features. The mirth was stolen from his smile. His eyes flicked back to gaze into the barn shadows. "Well...they have, I mean."

"What?" It was Chuck's turn to be lost in the conversation.

"He's awake! He's awake! Hey! He is awake!" The other voice crooned. Laughter followed after it. Then other sources of laughter joined in from the dark gloom and surrounded the two men.

"What's going on? What do you want, sir? I apologize for cursing at you. You upset me when you came close to my truck. That's all. I am sorry!" He was earnest. *Just want to go home.*

"Don't worry. I'm not mad. It's all part of the deal. I'm Neal by the way. You are?" he asked.

"Chuck. Chuck Broward."

"Ooooo Charlie! Charlie! Charlie!" The other voices filled the air.

"Hey, Chuck. You see, man, you chose the wrong night. You chose the wrong person to vent on. I mean, shit, lucky for me, but, yeah, shit deal for you." He stopped, turned toward the dark building again, and whistled.

At first, only the reflection of a pair of eyes could be seen. They were an odd faint blue. Then another pair of eyes opened, followed by two more behind it. They gathered together in the dark.

Chuck gasped in terror when a small, thin gray creature crept out of the gloom of the barn. It had a tiny, softball-sized skull, with fish-belly white skin stretched very tight over it. It didn't have a nose but a wide maw that spanned the entire skull. The mouth was filled with tubular teeth, translucent and very pointed. A pair of gray and pink tongues flashed snakelike in and out. Its eyes were solid, white buttons in the light. They were surrounded by triangular patches of red flesh that pulsated in obscure rhythms. The wolf-size beast crawled on two legs but had three sets of arms, the smallest near to the face, obviously meant for feeding scraps to the mouth.

"What the fuck is that?" Chuck cried out.

"Dinner guests! Dinner guests! Dinner guests!" Cried another of the beasts as it followed the first toward him. Even more were slowly emerging from the barn.

Another climbed out of the passenger side window of the GMC. It was broader than the others. Its back had two rows of small, ebony spikes sticking up from its skin. It said, "We accept! We accept! We accept your exchange, Neal!"

Glumly, Neal took one last long pull from his cigarette and snuffed it out under his boot. He glanced again at Chuck who was trembling and gasping for air. "I am really sorry, too. Like you said, man, I have family, and I want to see her again too. Shit deal for you. Sorry."

"Chuck! Chuck! Chuck!" they taunted. "Bad driver! Bad driver! Bad temper! But is he sweet? He he he! Sweet to eat? We shall see!"

Neal walked past the streaming horde of beasts as they crept out of the shadows and the barn. From his jacket he retrieved some earbuds and settled in behind the wheel of his van.

He refused to look up until the meal was done.

# THE LONG STRETCH  BY DEREK BARTON

Kris woke up with a start. Bright lights above him stung his eyes. His mouth was sand dry, and his throat felt swollen. As his vision adapted, he looked all about him. He was behind the steering wheel in his dark blue Thunderbird. It was smoothly running at idle.

He checked the rearview mirror. His short-cropped platinum-blonde hair was still well-groomed, and nothing seemed out of place. However, his slate-gray eyes were bloodshot and red-rimmed. He looked down at his light blue suit. It was relatively fresh, and he didn't note any wrinkles. He decided he hadn't been asleep long.

Ahead of the car, he could see a long empty road.

*Oh, it's the tunnel! The I-21,* Kris realized. It was what the locals in Clear Lake, Texas, called The Long Stretch. The tunnel was on his normal drive to work. He had recently been promoted to Operations Manager of a Healthcare Plan Center. On a normal day, the commute took about thirty-five minutes, most of it in this tunnel.

*God! I fell asleep. How the hell did I manage to do that?* he wondered.

He also found it odd that he couldn't recall the night before. Was he drinking? He hadn't had a black-out session in quite some time, but it wasn't off the table. His love of Bourbon was infamous. Sherry, his wife despised his "only vice" and gave him a shitstorm routinely over it.

He shrugged and put the car in Drive. There was no other traffic in front or behind him in the tunnel. His watch was missing, but he guessed it was near 5:00 AM. He found himself to be quite hungry and thirsty. The BP

Gas Station near the office would likely have some hot coffee and maybe a few donuts.

Kris patted his suit pants pockets, but they were empty. Shitty time to lose his wallet and cell phone. He sighed, disgusted with himself. It must've been a real party for him to walk out without his items.

*Did I party? Or did Sherry and I fight again, and I drank away my anger? Why the hell was this drive taking so long? Where's the exit?* His thoughts began to focus on the tunnel.

While he had driven inside it nearly twenty times this month alone, there were no details he could recall. It was constructed with a plain, black tar road. There were high gray concrete walls on either side of three wide lanes and a bike lane. White hanging LED lamps were every thirty feet.

The tunnel went on and on.

*Something's wrong. The tunnel portion of the drive is only twenty minutes or so tops. I've been over a half hour already.*

He looked at the odometer. Christ! It was way more than he remembered. 56312. Maybe a good four or five hundred more miles than he would have guessed.

*Was it a road trip and an end-all-be-all drunkfest? What the fuck? Sherry is going to tear me a new one when I get home tonight.* He shook his head. Then he realized he wasn't hung over either. He didn't even have a headache. His thoughts, though, were a bit foggy.

After driving for an hour, he pulled to the side and parked in the bike lane. He punched the button for the Hazard lights.

He then opened the glove compartment looking for his phone. In it, stuffed on the left side was a silver flip phone, maybe one of the old Motorolas. It was not his IPhone 13. There was nothing else in the compartment. His registration paperwork and insurance papers were all missing.

He retrieved the phone and examined it. It was fully charged, and had the current time of 3:52 AM on it as well as the date 9/18/2029, but nothing else on the display. There were no contacts listed. He checked the history and only one listed number had been called. It wasn't familiar, but he dialed it anyway.

It rang three times before an automated robotic voice answered. "Kristopher Anthony Todd. Pending. 23 days."

It disconnected without even prompting him to leave a voicemail message.

*Pending what? And what did it mean by 23 days?*

Starting to feel anxious, and with his temper beginning to boil, he again put the car in Drive. It was time to find the freaking exit!

Another hour passed in The Long Stretch. Kris swore the ceiling was lowering and the lanes were getting narrower. The world was crushing in on him. When the odometer hit 56412 — another hundred miles since he first checked -- he hit the brakes and screamed in helplessness. He pounded his fists on the dash so hard that a crack suddenly formed and split the smooth rubbery surface.

"Goddamn it! Where am —"

A flash of memory cut his thoughts off. Sherry was next to the dresser in their master bedroom. She was standing in a pink and purple pajama top and panties, combing out her long, auburn hair. He was coming out of the bathroom, shouting and stumbling. He was very drunk. His shirt was unbuttoned and it had fresh drink stains. She was screaming, "I am sick of your lies!"

He had screamed, "Shut that bitch mouth!" right before he swung wildly and punched her. She flew back sprawled across the bed.

Guilt and shame washed over his features. So, they did fight. He did get drunk and that's why he could not remember.

Yet something nagged at him. The memory seemed distant. *Wasn't that months ago?* he questioned himself.

Kris pressed hard on the gas pedal. No one was around so he got close to 110 on the speedometer. He was going to get to the damn exit, and he was going to get there now!

An hour and a half passed. Nothing in the tunnel had changed. No other cars appeared. He was starting to question whether he even woke that morning. Starting to question his sanity.

Eventually, the Thunderbird sputtered and then stalled, coasting to a stop. It was drained of battery power. He opened the door and walked in front of the car with his hands on his hips as he tried to figure out what to do next.

*The dent is gone!* His inner voice shouted at him. This wasn't his car after all! It was only the same make and model. He looked at the key fob and popped the trunk.

A thick, red stained carpet was rolled up and filled the majority of the trunk space. Tufts of auburn hair spilled out from the top. Blood had pooled and congealed by the taillight.

He gasped in shock and leaped back.

*No!*

He peered inside once more. The horrifying image had ghosted. There wasn't a body.

Inside was actually an interesting treasure trove of items. There was a package of bottled water next to a rolled-up sleeping bag. A camouflaged backpack had foodstuffs and a copy of The Green Mile by Stephen King, one of his favorite novels.

He shook his head, burying the ghastly image he thought he saw.

Nervously, he joked, "Well, we have everything we need, Dorothy. Let's follow that yellow brick road after all!"

Kris took the items and as many of the water bottles as he could cram in the sleeping bag and backpack.

Another instant vision exploded inside his mind. Sherry was in the backyard running. The side of her face and neck were bleeding profusely from deep slashes. He was also running, covered in blood.

The blood was not his.

He stood there shaking. The nightmare memory hit him hard at his core. "What did I do, babe? Oh God..."

He started walking again trying to clear his thoughts of the vision.

Kris struck his palm against his temple. He could call for help with the flip phone!

He dialed their house, praying she was alright and could answer the phone. Another robotic voice answered instead.

"The phone number you have dialed is invalid. Please check—"

Kris hung up, cursing and muttering under his breath. He dialed his work.

"The phone number you have dialed—"

Dialed his mother.

"The—"

How about this? He punched in 9 1 1.

"The phone number you have dialed is invalid. Please check your number and try again."

Sighing loudly, he called the only number that seemed to work. The robotic message came back on again.

"Kristopher Anthony Todd. Pending. 39 days."

Kris scoffed. He had no idea what it all meant and continued his hike.

At one point, he stopped and camped in the bike lane. He slept five hours on the cold tarmac, but his sleep was filled with chaotic, frantic dreams.

The infinite road went on and on. His feet blistered from the dress shoes. He ditched his suit jacket and his blue tie.

Seven hours later he made another stop to sleep. The cell phone told him: "Kristopher Anthony Todd. Pending. 47 days."

At 4:12 PM the next day, he spotted something new! It was at first only a dark and square object. After he managed to walk closer, he realized it was the same car he had abandoned. The trunk was still wide open.

Kris sank to his knees, broken and exhausted. *How is this happening? Why is this happening? What do—*

A tall slender man opened the driver's door and climbed out. He wore a blue jumpsuit with a black leather belt. Under a police officer's hat, the light-skinned man had on large reflecting sunglasses. His face had almost no clear shapes or details. He was blocky, similar to one of those people his nephew would make in his Minecraft video games. However, in the man's right hand, he carried a black pistol.

Kris lunged and bolted back down the roadway. He pulled out the cell again.

He dialed by reflex 9 1 1.

An actual human answered this time. A serious, but pleasant female voice said, "State the nature of your emergency please."

"Please! Please help me," he shouted, panting from his exertion.

"State the nature of your emergency please."

"I'm being chased. He has a gun! I don't know why or where I am!"

"Prisoner 56312, Kristopher Anthony Todd. Sentenced into CRIOSYS PENITENTIARY 65 days ago. Final appeal DENIED. Your execution date has been approved and moved to today 9/18/2029. Please remain still."

"FUCK YOU, LADY!" He screamed back and threw the phone hard to the ground.

The past year of arrest, court, press conferences, prison, images of Sherry's corpse — all rushed back to him. He had been charged and sentenced to die for killing his wife, Sherry Diane Todd almost a year ago. On Death Row, he had been forced into a new experimental AI-generated prison called CRIOSYS PENITENTIARY.

Kris didn't care about anything at that moment. He only ran. He knew he had to. His body may be lying in some cold storage, but his mind and soul were here in The Long Stretch! To live again, he couldn't stop running. He wouldn't!

The eruption of the gun, two blasts, the shock of the sounds, and the agonizing bloody holes opening in his chest struck him all at once.

Kristopher Anthony Todd's case was no longer Pending.

## THERE'S SOMETHING IN THE BASEMENT    BY T.D. BARTON

"Are you out of your mind?" Riley stared at Tommy Mahoney as though there was definite doubt about his sanity.

"What?" Mahoney replied, scratching at the stubble sprinkled over his narrow chin. He raised his glass and took a long swallow of beer. A jukebox warbled out a country tune from across the barroom as his Adam's Apple bobbed up and down in a matching rhythm.

"You know damn well what," his friend responded. "That place is haunted. Has been for generations. You'll never be safe there, much less comfortable."

Mahoney scoffed and rolled his eyes. "Come on Riles, you know I don't believe in that stuff. I never have. The price was right and well, I love the place. It has — atmosphere. The house was built in eighteen thirty-six. Think of it. I'm the owner of a house that was built before the Civil War. How cool is that? The place has a history." His almond-shaped eyes sparkled with excitement and self-assurance.

Riley hadn't touched his beer since Mahoney gave him the news. Riley Skinner was born in Lancaster and moved to Putnam when he was eight years old. He and Tommy Mahoney had met in the third grade and the two had been best friends ever since. Inseparable all through high school, Tommy had gone off to college after graduation while Riley stayed and went to work at his father's hardware store. Soon he would be the owner, as his father was nearing retirement. He had married and had two young children while Tommy had gone on to become a successful writer. There was no jealousy or resentment on either part as both were quite happy with their own lives and each was happy with his friend's success.

Now Tommy had returned home to Putnam and, according to what he had just told Riley, had purchased a house on the edge of town. The house was a three-story monstrosity in the Gothic-Revival style. It had a long history of owners and renters going back farther than anyone alive could remember. After all these years, it still had a solid foundation but desperately needed restoration.

"Oh, it has a history alright," moaned Riley, and his bushy eyebrows shot up to nearly meet his tousled red hair. "A history of death — both murder and suicide." He stared incredulously at his friend, who said nothing. "Everybody knows the place is haunted. Why would you want to live there?"

Mahoney smiled and shrugged his shoulders. "It's my kinda place," he said. "You know my great uncle Travis Mahoney was the last owner. When he died, the place sat vacant for thirty-three years until some realtors over in Lancaster took it over. I think they were planning on tearing it down until I came along. What a waste that would've been!"

Riley shook his head in disbelief and finally lifted his drink for a swallow. "You're nuts," he said.

"Look, I know it's going to take a lot of work and money for repairs, but I like the challenge. And once I have it put in shape it's gonna be great. What a place to work from, eh? The ideas will literally come out of the woodwork in an old house like that."

"That's not all that's going to come out of the woodwork," Riley grumbled. "You'll be up to your ears in spooks and haunts. I wouldn't be caught dead in that old place."

Mahoney had noticed the house was up for sale the day he returned to town. Tommy remembered all the stories about hauntings and spirits that had surrounded it since he was a child in grade school. All the kids avoided coming near the place, especially around Halloween time. They all thought it was creepy and scary and nothing to be messed with.

But little Tommy Mahoney found the house to be fascinating. He loved the way it looked with its steep-pitched roof and scalloped trim around gables, windows, and doors. The windows themselves were topped off with distinctive pointed arches. And a fabulous round portico graced the front of the weathered old home.

But more than the physical features, he felt the house exuded mystery and charm. He longed to get to know her, to uncover her secrets, and to revive the past that was buried within her walls. The place seemed to call to him to come inside, to touch, to feel, to become part of the history that belonged there. She was empty and alone, much like Tommy himself. She was crying out for life and for someone to bring a spark back to the dusty old structure. The house longed to share her saga of the past and her hopes for the future. As a child, he had vowed to someday own her and now he was determined to be the one to bring her back to life. And maybe to write her story.

The building was originally constructed by a man named Theodore Hartwell, who had made his fortune in lumber and imported goods. Hartwell had it built for his young wife Vanessa as a wedding present. They were very much in love, despite their age difference and all the signs pointed to a happy future.

However, after three years they remained childless, and a strain was being put on their relationship. Theo was patient and understanding but couldn't hide his disappointment. While Vanessa became despondent over her lack of fertility and after a time, arguments began to wedge the couple apart. The disagreements grew more and more frequent. Unable to reconcile their differences, they gave up on their efforts to reproduce and began sleeping in separate bedrooms.

It was during this time that Theo began dabbling in the dark arts. Ouija board demonstrations and seances were held there regularly with mediums called in from all around the country. And there were rumors of secret ceremonies being held within the depths of the place. But none of that was ever proven.

Then it was in the spring of eighteen forty-two that Vanessa inexplicably became pregnant with a long-awaited child. Unfortunately, Theo realized that the baby could not possibly be his. Although his pride was assaulted, the man so longed for a son he determined to never breach the subject with his wife and to raise the child as his own.

The couple continued as man and wife in name only occupying different beds up until the day the infant was to be born. Theo was overjoyed when his wife went into labor, but his happiness was short-lived as neither the mother nor the child survived the birthing.

It was a mere three days after the funerals that Theodore Hartwell, lumber baron, and recent widower hung himself by the neck from a beam in the basement. Unfortunately, because he lived alone, having dismissed all the servants, his decaying corpse was not found for three weeks.

The house sat abandoned for twelve years after that until it was purchased by the Stifflers, a family new to the area and unaware of the grisly background. In those days, realtors were not required to divulge such unsavory details to their prospective buyers. And so, it was months before they were informed through overheard gossip about the sad events.

Several heated discussions between husband and wife followed, bickering over whether or not to remain in the home. Mr. Stiffler was determined to keep the house and overruled his wife's objections. So, The Stifflers, all twelve of them, stayed in the house until Mr. Stiffler tripped at the top of the stairs, and was found dead on the hardpacked dirt floor of the cellar.

Again, the house was vacated. The Stiffler family, minus the head of the household, all moved back to Georgia. There, the children were separated to be doled out to various relatives.

The following families and various single owners over the years all had incidents. Someone either vanished under mysterious circumstances or was found dead. Eventually, the house had such a reputation that no one would even consider purchasing the property. Therefore, it sat empty up until last Monday when Tommy Mahoney bought it from an astonished Gene Hargrove, agent for Cranston Realty in Lancaster. It had been offered at an incredible price.

The door screeched loudly on rusted hinges as Tommy entered the front hall. To say the house had an unlived-in look would be an understatement. Years of neglect had left the place in a state that would have changed the average buyer's mind instantly. But Tommy was motivated and as he gazed around the dusty cobwebbed empty rooms he smiled with anticipation. There was a vision living in his head and he could picture exactly what the place would look like someday.

His footsteps echoed as he walked across the wooden floor in the living room and through the dining room. Most of the furniture had been sold at auction following the previous owner's death thirty-three years prior. But an enormous oak dining table remained surrounded by worn-looking chairs. *This whole set will have to be replaced,* Tommy thought as he ran his fingertips through the dust coating the tabletop.

In the kitchen, he noticed the uneven flooring and an enormous antique cast-iron stove. It was designed to burn wood or coal and connected to the ceiling with a black stovepipe. He considered it for a few moments and then shook his head. No, that would have to go as well. Tommy planned to strip the place down and start fresh. His latest book had put him in a financial position that would allow him to build his dream house and he wasn't going to be scrimping on anything.

After about half an hour he had toured the entire house and mapped out ideas in his head. It was time to start bringing things in from the black Ram truck he'd parked in the cobbled driveway. Riley had offered to let him stay at his house the first night, but Tommy politely declined. "I have an air mattress, toiletries, food, and supplies — everything I need, and the new furniture and appliances are scheduled to arrive tomorrow," he said. "I can't wait to start moving in."

When Riley looked skeptical, Tommy held up his hand and said, "I'll be alright, trust me."

The cabinets in the kitchen weren't serviceable and Tommy was somewhat concerned about mice or rats. And so, he simply lined up canned goods and boxes on the counter beside the sink. He twisted the tap and was pleased to see the water had been turned on. It was brown at first but soon coughed repeatedly and began to run clear. He flipped the ancient light switch on the wall and saw that the power had yet to be connected. No worries. Tommy had flashlights. Another trip to the truck added a large cooler filled with ice. This should suffice for perishables.

Tommy visited the truck several more times and soon he had made himself comfortable for the night. It wasn't quite up to twenty-first-century standards, but when darkness fell, he lit an old Coleman lantern and placed it by his makeshift bed. This made him think of the time in which the house had been built.

With a sigh, the author stretched out on the mattress and began re-reading the outline of a story he was currently working on. He wasn't sure whether it was going to be a subject worthy of another novel or maybe only a short story or novella. Either way, he felt it was an idea worth fleshing out.

Sometime later he awoke with a start and wondered where he was. The hissing sound of the kerosene lantern filled the room, but its meager light fell way short of illuminating the large dark living area. It was a moonless night, and the thick dusty glass of the windows didn't help to brighten things. For a few moments, Tommy was disoriented. He shook his head and stared around the room trying to pierce the darkness.

At length, it all came back to him, and he understood where he was and was chagrined to realize he had fallen asleep with the lantern burning. He held it up over his head and looked around the room. His fuzzy mind asked why he had suddenly awakened. Had he heard a noise? Again, he surveyed the dark room.

With a wry smile and a chuckle, he thought, *"Of course I heard a noise. It would be impossible not to hear noises in an old house like this."* Tommy shook his head and checked his Apple watch for the time. It read 01:13. He sighed loudly and settled back down on the mattress.

Rolling over onto his side, Tommy turned the lantern down and blackness enveloped the room. Without the hum of modern appliances or air conditioning, the house was as silent as a tomb. It was unsettling to lie there with total darkness filling the room and nothing to hear except his breath and the beating of his heart. In the old movies, a storm always rages outside with thunder booming and lightning flashing. The howling of wind would also add to the spooky atmosphere. But somehow this silence was worse. It took Tommy a long time before he drifted off to sleep once more.

The next time he woke was far more frightening than the first time. He started up from a disturbing dream with the distinct feeling that someone was leaning over inches from his face. Tommy sat bolt upright and emitted a strangled scream. Complete darkness muffled his senses, and a low scraping sound came from somewhere in the house, accompanied by someone sobbing bitterly. He couldn't be sure, but that's what it sounded like. The noises seemed to come from all around and in contrast to the previous hush, it was very loud. Hands shaking, he thrashed around trying to find a flashlight so that he could relight the Coleman.

At last, the back of his hand brushed something hard lying beside the mattress and he grabbed it, recognizing it as the flashlight. He fumbled for a second or two trying to find the switch. Meanwhile, the scraping, moaning, sobbing sound was growing louder and seemed to be coming closer. It was a cold, slobbery noise that caused the skin on Tommy's arms and neck to prickle in gooseflesh.

The instant he flipped on the flashlight and started waving it wildly around the room, the sound stopped. Tommy probed the darkness in the far corners and out into the connecting rooms. There was nothing to be seen.

He pulled a lighter from the pocket of his jeans and relit the Coleman. Tommy stood up. He held the lantern high and walked out into the dining room. Still, there was nothing to be seen. At last, he gave up and decided it had all been a nasty dream that had dragged him from a fitful sleep, and he turned back toward his mattress. He told himself this but was not completely convinced.

As he lay back down, fully clothed, he was surprised at how cold the room had gotten. Pulling a blanket from one of his suitcases, Tommy crawled beneath it, fluffed his pillow, and told himself to relax. This time, however, he left the lantern burning on purpose.

When he was finally drifting off to sleep a loud banging noise came from the kitchen and Tommy was immediately on his feet. He grasped the lantern with one hand and picked up the flashlight with the other. Slowly he approached the kitchen while the loud knocking sound continued. It sounded like someone pounding furiously on a door somewhere. The sound came in groups of three. Bang! Bang! Bang! Then a short pause followed by another series of Bang! Bang! Bang! It was very solid, very physical, like the sound of a rock-hard fist.

Tommy entered the kitchen, and the sound became even louder. His flashlight picked out a locked door near the stove that Tommy assumed was the door to the cellar. He approached the door with understandable trepidation and then, as he stood before it, the knocking stopped. But below his feet, deep in the bowels of the old house the scraping, moaning sobbing sound began again.

*"There's something in the basement,"* Tommy thought to himself. And then, in a voice choked with fear he said aloud, "There's something in the basement."

Tommy's logic had always refused to accept the idea of ghosts or goblins, and, before he had the chance to change his mind, he threw back the bolt lock with a flourish and flung open the door.

He shined the beam down into the silent depths of the cellar and listened. There was nothing to be seen, nothing to be heard. Only silence and stygian darkness lay beyond the door. After some time, he placed his foot on the first step and slowly followed with his other foot. Bending slightly at the waist, he held the lantern aloft and peered into the darkness.

As he raised his foot to go lower, something grabbed his leg and flung him off out of balance, causing him to tumble down the stairs and land face-first on the hard-packed earth of the floor below. As he fell, something cold seemed to rush by him, up the stairs and out the cellar door. It was dark like a shadow, but somehow more solid and tangible, and yet at the same time ethereal.

When Tommy came to, he had no idea how long he had been out. He found himself again in pitch blackness and he felt sticky blood and dirt covering his face. Gingerly he felt for wounds and found blood still trickling from his scalp.

He spat dirt from between his cracked lips and began feeling about for the flashlight or perhaps the lantern. At last, he located the Coleman and lit it. It must have gone out when he fell because it still contained a good fuel supply. Using the lantern he found the flashlight. It had come apart and lay in pieces on the floor. Tommy screwed it back together and was relieved to see that it still worked.

He shone the beam around the room and saw various boxes and old wooden crates lining the walls. Dust-covered canned goods were on a rough-cut wooden shelf and spider webs were strung everywhere, connecting forgotten relics of the past. Above was a wooden ceiling with bare beams covered in more webbing. From one of the beams hung a short piece of ancient-looking rope.

Pulling himself to his feet, Tommy climbed slowly up the stairs but found the door either jammed or somehow locked again. He shoved and pounded against it with all his might, but it would not yield. At last, he turned around and went back into the cellar. At this point, he decided to turn off the flashlight to save the batteries. Who knew how long he was going to be stuck down here? His smartphone was not showing any signal, maybe it had been damaged in the fall, or perhaps simply couldn't make a connection down here.

Exploring the basement with the lantern, Tommy was surprised to discover how many ancient items littered the area. There was an old plow of the horse-drawn variety. Rotted water barrels, a broken-down grandfather clock, an old butter churn, all these things, and more were stashed away down here. It was almost as though nothing had changed since the old days when the house had been originally built and abandoned.

It occurred to him that, in a house this old there might be a coal chute or at least some old casement windows. Ignoring the roaring pain in his head and the throbbing of his damaged face, he moved slowly around the room looking for an alternative way out.

Tomy spent a long time searching but had no luck. At some point, he decided he needed to rest. He knew that he had lost a lot of blood, and his energy was quickly fading. Dragging one last heavy wooden crate out from the wall, he looked behind it for a coal chute. Then dizziness overcame him, and he collapsed in the space between the wall and the crate. Even with the lantern still burning, darkness enveloped him.

Riley decided a week was long enough. He hadn't heard anything from his friend and Tommy wasn't answering his calls. It was time to investigate. As much as he dreaded going into that house, he was forced to check it out. If something happened to Tommy, it would be like losing a brother.

The floorboards creaked beneath his weight as Riley walked across the front porch. There was a note on the door from the moving company. According to the note, they had attempted to deliver a truckload of furniture only to find the place locked up and nobody home. The note had a hostile tone. The company would be charging for delivery, regardless of reason or excuses.

Riley knocked on the entrance, but there was no response. He attempted to open the door, but it was locked. He walked around and peered through a window. The interior of the house was dark, but Riley thought he could make out some bedding in the middle of the living room. It would appear that Tommy had at least been here. His truck was in the driveway.

Riley walked around to the side of the house and looked through another window. He circled to the back yard but the door there was locked as well. Riley didn't know what to do. He was beginning to worry. Why had Tommy bought this old place? He had tried to warn him. Riley returned to the front door and made up his mind. He was going to have to force his way in. He would gladly pay for any repairs to be sure that Tommy was alright.

With a grimace, Riley raised a booted foot and slammed it against the heavy door. It remained closed. After the third try, the door facing splintered, and the door swung in with a bang.

"Tommy!" Riley called as he entered the room. He looked around and was appalled by the appearance of the place. *"This couldn't be more of a cliché for a haunted house,"* he thought. And again, he wondered what his friend had been thinking. "Hey, bud!" he yelled, and the echo resounded around the room. "Where are you, Mahoney?"

Nothing but silence.

Riley gazed down at the mattress and blanket on the floor. It was evident that Tommy had slept there, but where was he now? With great trepidation, Riley forced himself to begin searching the drafty old house.

When Tommy came to, the light was gone again. He groped around the floor for the lantern but found nothing. Continuing to search the room, he wondered how long he had been out this time. In the pitch-black silence of this cursed cellar, it was impossible to measure time. He could have been unconscious for an hour or a week, there was no way to tell. Despite his attempts to remain calm, panic was beginning to well up inside him. He brushed his hands frantically through the dirt looking for the flashlight. Suddenly, he felt it there in the dark. It was lying beside something that felt like a piece of cloth with a human limb inside of it.

With a gasp, he grabbed the light and switched it on. To his horror, the beam fell on a dead body leaning up against a wooden crate. The body looked as though it had been there for days at least, maybe more. With trembling hands, he shone the shaky beam in the face of the corpse.

He didn't recognize it at first because it was horribly mangled and covered with dried blood and dirt. But after a few moments, it dawned on him that there was something familiar about its features. Playing the beam over the body he caught sight of something that caused him to drop the flashlight and run in terror back up the stairs. It was his Apple watch, covered in dust dangling from the cold dead wrist.

Tragically, he now understood that he was dead and bled to death in the corner. His soul had left his body, and he had joined the long line of owners of this house who had died in the cellar.

Sobbing in anguish, Tommy scraped his nails against the still-locked door. Over and over, he scratched at the splintery old wood. Then he began to pound at it in frustration. Bang! Bang! Bang! *"Let me out,"* he cried. *"Please, Let me out! I don't want to spend eternity down here. Let me out!"* Bang! Bang! Bang!

"*You can't get out,*" came an ethereal voice behind him. When he turned, Tommy was amazed to see a fine wispy mist floating in the room's far corner. As he watched, fascinated, the mist began to swirl and gradually congeal into the shape of a bearded man, dressed in old-fashioned garb. The man spoke again. His voice was thin and raspy but held an air of authority that could not be denied.

"*It was I who built this domicile,*" *he said. "I am the first to live here and I was the first to die in this cellar.*" *He turned his gaze to the rope dangling from the beam in the middle of the room. "I lived alone, and I died alone. And since I died by my own hand, my spirit was cursed to remain within the confines of this room throughout eternity --- alone. This was the hell that was assigned to me.*"

These words spilled from the mouth of the thing that had been Theodore Hartwell past lips that never moved. His voice was as ice-cold and cruel as wind pouring over a snow-capped mountain summit. His eyes glowed with an eerie blue fire within and carried not the slightest hint of compassion nor emotion of any kind. What he was saying was as solid and unchangeable as time. The word had been spoken and so would it be. Tommy remained quiet as Hartwell continued.

"*But upon my death, with the final words choking from my throat, I uttered a curse of my own. Forever forward, whosoever enters this cellar and dies within, their souls shall be bound within these walls. Their souls will be doomed to remain in limbo along with mine until such time they secure a replacement. At that moment the door shall be unlocked, and their spirit may be free to move on. In life, I was denied a family, loved ones, or offspring. And so, the replacement must be someone they love --- a family member, trusted friend, or a descendant. That person then will inherit the curse until such time as they unlock the door.*"

"Why would you cast such an unholy curse, you bitter old man?" the ghost of Tommy asked. But no reply came back, and Hartwell's spirit faded into black.

After a time, Tommy turned his attention back to the door.

The banging and weeping sounds were coming from a door in the kitchen. There were muffled words, but Riley couldn't make them out through the heavy wood. By this time, he was terrified. His heart was pounding, and his palms were soaked in sweat. He stood before the door and stared at it, unable to move. The last thing Riley Skinner wanted to do was to open that creepy old door. God only knew what kind of terror lay on the other side.

But then again, what if it was Tommy knocking on that door, maybe he had accidentally locked himself in another room. Perhaps he was injured. Riley couldn't simply abandon him out of fear.

Against everything inside that warned him not to do it, Riley released the lock and eased the door open. He felt around for a light switch but there was nothing to relieve the darkness below. Shaking badly, he stepped down and felt something cold rush past and bump against his leg. To his utter horror, he found himself falling down the dark stairway and landing hard on a dirt floor. At the top of the stairs, the door slammed shut and utter darkness surrounded him.

Tommy's spirit hurtled out from the prison. In a blind rush, he hurled himself through the open door and slammed it closed.

"Tommy!" Riley cried out in the darkness. "Was that you?"

The lock fell into place! As his spirit faded away toward the afterlife, Tommy realized who it was that had released him from limbo. Despite his regrets, he knew he could not go back and change what he had done. He had sacrificed his best friend for his own freedom. Riley would now take his place beside the lonely old man who so wanted a son. And he would remain there until the day when he could lure some other unfortunate soul to their doom. That could be a long, long time. "I'm sorry, Riles," he thought. "So sorry. It looks like you *will* be found dead in this old house after all." It was the last earthly thought Tommy Mahoney ever had before his consciousness drifted away and joined with the universe. Once again, the tired old house was filled with silence. But in the basement, something waited.

"Are you out of your mind?" Riley stared at Tommy Mahoney as though there was definite doubt about his sanity. He hadn't touched his beer since Mahoney gave him the news.

"What?" Mahoney replied, scratching at the stubble sprinkled over his narrow chin. He raised his glass and took a long swallow of beer. A jukebox warbled out a country tune from across the barroom as his Adam's Apple bobbed up and down.

"You know damn well what," his friend responded. "That place is haunted. Has been for generations. You'll never be safe there, much less comfortable."

Mahoney scoffed and rolled his eyes. "Come on Riles, you know I don't believe in that stuff. I never have. The price was right and well, I love the place. It has -- atmosphere. The house was built in eighteen thirty-six. Think of that. I'm the owner of a house that was built before the Civil War. How cool is that? The place has history." His almond-shaped eyes sparkled with excitement and self-assurance.

Riley Skinner had been born in Lancaster and moved to Putnam when he was just eight years old. He and Tommy Mahoney had met in the third grade and the two men had been best friends ever since. Inseparable all through high school, Tommy had gone off to college after graduation and Riley stayed and went to work at his father's hardware store. Soon he would be the owner, as his father was nearing retirement. He had married and had two young children while Tommy had gone on to become a successful writer. There was no jealousy or resentment on either part as both were quite happy with their own lives and each was happy with his friend's success.

Now Tommy had returned home to Putnam and, according to what he had just told Riley, had purchased a house on the edge of town. The house was a three-story monstrosity in the Gothic-Revival style that had a long history of owners and renters going back farther than anyone alive could remember. After all these years, it still had a solid foundation but was in dire need of restoration.

"Oh, it has a history alright," moaned Riley, and his bushy eyebrows shot up to nearly meet his tousled black hair. "A history of death -- both murder and suicide." He stared incredulously at his friend, who said nothing. "Everybody knows the place is haunted. Why would you want to live there?"

Mahoney smiled and shrugged his shoulders. "It's my kinda place," he said. "You know my great uncle Travis Mahoney was the last owner. When he died, the place sat vacant for thirty-three years until some realtors over in Lancaster took it over. I think they were planning on tearing it down until I came along. What a waste that would've been!"

Riley shook his head in disbelief and finally lifted his drink for a swallow. "You're nuts." He said.

"Look, I know it's going to take a lot of work and money for repairs, but I like the challenge. And once I have it put in shape it's gonna be great. What a place to work from, eh? The ideas will literally come out of the woodwork in an old house like that."

"That's not all that's going to come out of the woodwork," Riley grumbled. "You'll be up to your ears in spooks and haunts. I wouldn't be caught dead in that old place."

Mahoney had noticed the house was up for sale the day he returned to town. Tommy remembered all the stories about hauntings and spirits that had surrounded it since he was a child in grade school. All the kids avoided coming near the place, especially around Halloween time. They all thought it was creepy and scary and nothing to be messed with.

But little Tommy Mahoney found the house to be fascinating. He loved the way it looked with its steep-pitched roof and scalloped trim around gables, windows, and doors. The windows themselves were topped off in distinctive pointed arches and a fabulous round portico graced the front of the weathered old home.

But more than the physical features, he felt the house exuded mystery and charm. He longed to get to know her, to uncover her secrets, and to revive the past that was buried within her walls. The place seemed to call to him to come inside, to touch, to feel, to become part of the history that belonged there. She was empty and alone, much like Tommy himself. She was crying out for life and for someone to bring a spark back to the dusty old structure. The house longed to share her saga of the past and her hopes for the future. As a child, he had vowed to someday own her and now he was determined to be the one to bring her back to life. And maybe to write her story.

The building was originally constructed by a man named Theodore Hartwell, who had made his fortune in lumber and imported goods. Hartwell had it built for his young wife Vanessa as a wedding present. They were very much in love, despite their age differences and all the signs pointed to a happy future.

However, after three years they remained childless, and a strain was being put on their relationship. Theo was patient and understanding but couldn't hide his disappointment. While Vanessa became despondent over her lack of fertility and after a time, arguments began to wedge the couple apart. The disagreements grew more and more frequent until, unable to reconcile their differences, they gave up on their efforts to reproduce and began sleeping in separate bedrooms.

It was during this time that Theo began dabbling in the dark arts. Ouija board demonstrations and seances were held there regularly with mediums called in from all around the country. And there were rumors of secret ceremonies being held within the depths of the place. But none of that was ever proven.

Then it was in the spring of eighteen forty-two that Vanessa inexplicably became pregnant with a long-awaited child. Unfortunately, Theo realized that the baby could not possibly be his. Although his pride was assaulted, the man so longed for a son he determined to never breach the subject with his wife and to raise the child as his own.

The couple continued as man and wife in name only occupying different beds up until the day the infant was to be born. Theo was overjoyed when his wife went into labor, but his happiness was short-lived as neither the mother nor the child survived the birthing.

It was a mere three days after the funerals that Theodore Hartwell, lumber baron, and recent widower hung himself by the neck from a beam in the basement. Unfortunately, because he lived alone, having dismissed all the servants, his decaying corpse was not found for three weeks.

The house sat abandoned for twelve years after that until it was purchased by the Stifflers, a family new to the area and unaware of the grisly background. In those days, realtors were not required to divulge such unsavory details to their prospective buyers. And so, it was months before they were informed through overheard gossip about the sad events.

Several heated discussions between husband and wife followed, bickering over whether or not to remain in the home. Mr. Stiffler was determined to keep the house and overruled his wife's objections. So, The Stifflers, all twelve of them, stayed in the house until Mr. Stiffler apparently tripped at the top of the stairs and wound up dead on the hardpacked dirt floor of the cellar.

Again, the house was vacated. The Stiffler family, minus the head of the household, all moved back to Georgia, where the children were separated to be doled out to various relatives.

The following families and various single owners over the years all had incidents where someone either vanished under mysterious circumstances or was found dead. Eventually, the house had such a reputation that no one would even consider purchasing it and so it sat empty up until last Monday when Tommy Mahoney bought it from an astonished Gene Hargrove, agent for Cranston Realty in Lancaster. It had been offered at an incredible price.


The door screeched loudly on rusted hinges as Tommy entered the front hall. To say the house had an unlived-in look would be an understatement. Years of neglect had left the place in a state that would have changed the average buyer's mind instantly. But Tommy was motivated and as he gazed around the dusty cobwebbed empty rooms he smiled with anticipation. There was a vision living in his head and he could picture exactly what the place would look like someday.

His footsteps echoed as he walked across the wooden floor in the living room and through the dining room. Most of the furniture had been sold at auction following the previous owner's death thirty-three years prior. But an enormous oak dining table remained surrounded by worn-looking chairs. *This whole set will have to be replaced,* Tommy thought as he ran his fingertips through the dust coating the tabletop.

In the kitchen, he noticed the uneven flooring and an enormous antique cast-iron stove designed to burn wood or coal and connected to the ceiling with a black stovepipe. He considered it for a few moments and then shook his head. No that would have to go as well. Tommy planned to strip the place down and start fresh. His latest book had put him in a financial position that would allow him to build his dream house and he wasn't going to be scrimping on anything.

After about half an hour he had toured the entire house and mapped out ideas in his head. It was time to start bringing things in from the black Ram truck he'd parked in the cobbled driveway. Riley had offered to let him stay at his house the first night, but Tommy politely declined. "I have an air mattress, toiletries, food, and supplies — everything I need, and the new furniture and appliances are scheduled to arrive tomorrow," he said. "I can't wait to start moving in."

When Riley looked skeptical, Tommy held up his hand and said, "I'll be alright, trust me."

The cabinets in the kitchen weren't really serviceable and Tommy was somewhat concerned about mice or rats, so he simply lined up canned goods and boxes on the counter beside the sink. He twisted the tap and was pleased to see the water had been turned on. It was brown at first but soon coughed repeatedly and began to run clear. He flipped the ancient light switch on the wall and saw that the power had yet to be connected. No worries. Tommy had flashlights. Another trip to the truck added a large cooler filled with ice. This should suffice for perishables.

Tommy visited the truck several more times and soon he had made himself comfortable for the night. It wasn't quite up to twenty-first-century standards, but when darkness fell, he lit an old Coleman lantern and placed it by his makeshift bed. This at least brought him even with the time in which the house had been built.

With a sigh, the author stretched out on the mattress and began re-reading the outline of a story he was currently working on. He wasn't sure whether it was going to be a subject worthy of another novel or maybe just a short story or novella. Either way, he felt it was an idea worth fleshing out.

Sometime later he awoke with a start and wondered where he was. The hissing sound of the kerosene lantern filled the room, but its meager light fell way short of illuminating the large dark living area. It was a moonless night, and the thick glass of the windows didn't help to brighten things. For a few moments, Tommy was disoriented. He shook his head and stared around the room trying to pierce the darkness.

At length, it all came back to him, and he understood where he was and was chagrined to realize he had fallen asleep with the lantern burning. He held it up over his head and looked around the room. His fuzzy mind asked why he had suddenly awakened. Had he heard a noise? Again, he surveyed the dark room.

With a wry smile and a chuckle, he thought, *"Of course I heard a noise. It would be impossible not to hear noises in an old house like this."* Tommy shook his head and checked his Apple watch for the time. It read 01:13. He sighed loudly and settled back down on the mattress.

Rolling over onto his side, Tommy turned the lantern down and blackness enveloped the room. Without the hum of modern appliances or air conditioning, the house was literally as silent as a tomb. It was unsettling to lie there with total darkness filling the room and nothing to hear except his breath and the beating of his heart. In the old movies, a storm always rages outside with thunder booming and lightning flashing. The howling of wind would also add to the spooky atmosphere. But somehow this silence was worse. It took Tommy a long time before he drifted off to sleep once more.

The next time he woke was far more frightening than the first time. He started up from a disturbing dream with the distinct feeling that someone was leaning over just inches from his face. Tommy sat bolt upright and emitted a strangled scream. Complete darkness muffled his senses, and a low scraping sound came from somewhere in the house accompanied by what sounded like someone sobbing bitterly. The sound seemed to come from all around and in contrast to the previous hush, it was very loud. Hands shaking, he thrashed around trying to find a flashlight so that he could relight the Coleman.

At last, the back of his hand brushed something hard lying beside the mattress and he grabbed it, recognizing it as the flashlight. He fumbled for a second or two trying to find the switch. Meanwhile, the scraping, moaning, sobbing sound was growing louder and seemed to be coming closer. It was a cold, slobbery noise that caused the skin on Tommy's arms and neck to prickle in gooseflesh.

The instant he flipped on the flashlight and started waving it wildly around the room, the sound stopped. Tommy probed the darkness in the far corners and out into the connecting rooms. There was nothing to be seen.

He pulled a lighter from the pocket of his jeans and relit the Coleman. Tommy stood up. He held the lantern high and walked out into the dining room. Still, there was nothing to be seen. At last, he gave up and decided it had all been a nasty dream that had dragged him from a fitful sleep, and he turned back toward his mattress. He told himself this but was definitely not completely convinced.

As he lay back down, fully clothed, he was surprised at how cold the room had gotten. Pulling a blanket from one of his suitcases, Tommy crawled beneath it, fluffed his pillow, and told himself to relax. This time, however, he left the lantern burning on purpose.

Just as he was finally drifting off to sleep a loud banging noise came from the kitchen and Tommy was immediately on his feet. He grasped the lantern with one hand and picked up the flashlight with the other. Slowly he approached the kitchen while the loud knocking sound continued. It sounded like someone pounding furiously on a door somewhere. The sound came in groups of three. Bang! Bang! Bang! Then a short pause followed by another series of Bang! Bang! Bang! It was very solid, very physical, like the sound of a rock-hard fist.

Tommy entered the kitchen, and the sound became even louder. His flashlight picked out a locked door near the stove that Tommy assumed was the door to the cellar. He approached the door with understandable trepidation and then, just as he stood before it the knocking stopped. But below his feet, deep in the bowels of the old house the scraping, moaning sobbing sound began again.

*"There's something in the basement,"* Tommy thought to himself. And then, in a voice choked with fear he said aloud, "There's something in the basement."

Tommy's logic had always refused to accept the idea of ghosts or goblins, and, before he could give himself time to change his mind, he threw back the bolt lock with a flourish and flung open the door.

He shined the beam down into the silent depths of the cellar and listened. There was nothing to be seen, nothing to be heard. Only silence and stygian darkness lay beyond the door. After some time, he placed his foot on the first step and slowly followed with his other foot. Bending slightly at the waist, he held the lantern aloft and peered into the darkness.

As he raised his foot to go lower, something grabbed his leg and flung him out of balance, causing him to tumble down the stairs and land face-first in the hard-packed earth of the floor below. As he fell, something cold seemed to rush by him, up the stairs and out the cellar door.

When Tommy came to, he had no idea how long he had been out. He found himself again in pitch blackness and he felt sticky blood and dirt covering his face. Gingerly he felt for wounds and found blood still trickling from his scalp.

He spat dirt from between his cracked lips and began feeling about for the flashlight or perhaps the lantern. At last, he located the Coleman and lit it. It must have gone out when he fell because it still contained a good fuel supply. Using the lantern he found the flashlight. It had come apart and lay in pieces on the floor. Tommy screwed it back together and was relieved to see that it still worked.

He shone the beam around the room and saw various boxes and old wooden crates lining the walls, dust-covered canned goods were on a rough-cut wooden shelf and spider webs were strung everywhere, connecting forgotten relics of the past. Above was a wooden ceiling with bare beams covered in more webbing. From one of the beams hung a short piece of ancient-looking rope.

Pulling himself to his feet, Tommy climbed slowly up the stairs but found the door either jammed or somehow locked again. He shoved and pounded against it with all his might, but it would not yield. At last, he turned around and went back into the cellar. At this point, he decided to turn off the flashlight to save the batteries. Who knew how long he was going to be stuck down here? His smartphone was not showing any signal, maybe it had been damaged in the fall, or perhaps just couldn't make a connection down here.

Exploring the basement, Tommy was surprised to discover how many ancient items littered the area. There was an old plow of the horse-drawn variety. Axes and hand drills, wood splitting tools, an old butter churn, all these things, and more were stashed away down here. It was almost as though nothing had changed since the old days when the house had been originally built and abandoned.

It occurred to him that, in a house this old there might be a coal chute or at least some old casement windows. Ignoring the roaring pain in his head and the throbbing of his damaged face, he moved slowly around the room looking for an alternative way out.

Tomy spent a long time searching but had no luck. At some point, he decided he needed to rest. He knew that he had lost a lot of blood, and his energy was quickly fading. Dragging one last heavy wooden crate out from the wall, he looked behind it for a coal chute. Then dizziness overcame him, and he collapsed in the space between the wall and the crate. Even with the lantern still burning, darkness enveloped him.

Riley decided a week was long enough. He hadn't heard anything from his friend and Tommy wasn't answering his calls. It was time to investigate. As much as he dreaded going into that house, he was forced to check it out. If something happened to Tommy, it would be like losing a brother.

The floorboards creaked beneath his weight as Riley walked across the front porch. There was a note on the door from the moving company. Apparently, they had attempted to deliver a truckload of furniture only to find the place locked up and nobody home. The note had a hostile air about it. The company would be charging for delivery, regardless of reason or excuses.

Riley knocked on the entrance, but there was no response. He attempted to open the door, but it was locked. He walked around and peered through a window. The interior of the house was dark, but Riley thought he could make out some bedding in the middle of the living room. It would appear that Tommy had at least been here. His truck was in the driveway.

Riley walked around to the side of the house and looked through another window. He circled to the back yard but the door there was locked as well. Riley didn't know what to do. He was really beginning to worry. Why had Tommy bought this old place? He had tried to warn him. Riley returned to the front door and made up his mind. He was going to have to force his way in. He would gladly pay for any repairs to be sure that Tommy was alright.

With a grimace, Riley raised a booted foot and slammed it against the heavy door. It remained closed. After the third try, the door facing splintered, and the door swung in with a bang.

"Tommy!" Riley called as he entered the room. He looked around and was appalled by the appearance of the place. *"This couldn't be more of a cliché for a haunted house,"* he thought. And again, he wondered what his friend had been thinking. "Hey, bud!" he yelled, and the echo resounded around the room. "Where are you, Mahoney?"

Nothing but silence.

Riley gazed down at the mattress and blanket on the floor. It was evident that Tommy had slept there, but where was he now? With great trepidation, Riley forced himself to begin searching the drafty old house.

When Tommy came to, the light was gone again. He groped around the floor for the lantern but found nothing. Continuing to search the room, he wondered how long he had been out this time. In the pitch-black silence of this cursed cellar, it was impossible to measure time. He could have been unconscious for an hour or a week, there was no way to tell. Despite his attempts to remain calm, panic was beginning to well up inside him, and he brushed his hands frantically through the dirt looking for the flashlight. Suddenly, he felt it there in the dark. It was lying beside something that felt like a piece of cloth with a human limb inside of it.

With a gasp, he grabbed the light and switched it on. To his horror, the beam fell on a dead body leaning up against a wooden crate. The body looked as though it had been there for days at least, maybe more. With trembling hands, he shone the shaky beam in the face of the corpse.

He didn't recognize it at first because it was horribly mangled and covered with dried blood and dirt. But after a few moments, it dawned on him that there was something familiar about its features. Playing the beam over the body he caught sight of something that caused him to drop the flashlight and run in terror back up the stairs. It was his Apple watch, covered in dust dangling from the cold dead wrist.

Tragically, he now understood that he was dead, bled to death in the corner. His soul had left his body and he had joined the long line of owners of this house who had died in the cellar.

Sobbing in anguish, Tommy scraped his nails against the still-locked door. Over and over, he scratched at the splintery old wood. Then he began to pound at it in frustration. Bang! Bang! Bang! *"Let me out,"* he cried. *"Please, Let me out! I don't want to spend eternity down here. Let me out!"* Bang! Bang! Bang!

*"You can't get out,"* came an ethereal voice behind him. When he turned, Tommy was amazed to see a fine wispy mist floating in the room's far corner. As he watched, fascinated, the mist began to swirl and gradually form the shape of a bearded man, dressed in old-fashioned garb. The man spoke again. His voice was thin and raspy but held an air of authority that could not be denied.

*"It was I who built this domicile,"* he said. *"I am the first to live here and I was the first to die in this cellar."* He turned his gaze to the rope dangling from the beam in the middle of the room. *"I lived alone, and I died alone. And since I died by my own hand, my spirit was cursed to remain within the confines of this room throughout eternity --- alone. This was the hell that was assigned to me."*

These words spilled from the mouth of the thing that had been Theodore Hartwell past lips that never moved. His voice was as ice-cold and cruel as wind pouring over a snow-capped mountain summit. His eyes glowed with an eerie blue fire within and carried not the slightest hint of compassion nor emotion of any kind. What he was saying was as solid and unchangeable as the sea. The word had been spoken and so would it be. Tommy remained quiet as Hartwell continued.

"But upon my death, with the final words choking from my throat, I uttered a curse of my own: Forever forward, whosoever enters this cellar and dies within, their souls shall be doomed to stay within its boundaries and keep me company. Their souls will be doomed to remain in limbo along with mine until such time they secure a replacement. At that moment the door shall be unlocked, and their spirit may be free to move on. In life, I was denied a family, loved ones, or offspring. And so, the replacement must be someone they love — a family member, trusted friend, or a descendant. That person then will inherit the curse until such time as they unlock the door."

"Why would you cast such an unholy curse, you bitter old man?" the ghost of Tommy asked. But no reply came back, and Hartwell's spirit faded into black.

After a time, Tommy turned his attention back to the door.

The banging and weeping sounds were coming from a door in the kitchen. There were muffled words, but Riley couldn't make them out through the heavy old door. By this time, he was terrified. His heart was pounding, and his palms were soaked in sweat. He stood before the door and stared at it, unable to move. The last thing Riley Skinner wanted to do was to open that creepy old door. God only knew what kind of terror lay on the other side.

But then again, what if it was Tommy knocking on that door, maybe he had accidentally locked himself in another room. Perhaps he was injured. Riley couldn't simply abandon him out of fear.

Against everything inside that warned him not to do it, Riley released the lock and eased the door open. He felt around for a light switch but there was nothing to relieve the darkness below. Shaking badly, he took a step down and felt something cold rush past and bump against his leg. To his utter horror, he found himself falling down the dark stairway and landing hard on a dirt floor. At the top of the stairs, the door slammed shut and utter darkness surrounded him.

Tommy's spirit hurtled out from the prison. In a blind rush, he hurled himself through the open door and slammed it closed.

"Tommy!" Riley cried out in the darkness. "Was that you?"

The lock fell into place and as his spirit began to fade away into the afterlife, Tommy realized who it was that had released him from limbo and, despite his regrets, he knew he could not go back and change what he had done. He had sacrificed his best friend for his own freedom. Riley would now take his place beside the lonely old man who so wanted a son. And he would remain there until the day when he could lure some other unfortunate soul to their doom. That could be a long, long time. "I'm sorry, Riles," he thought. "So sorry. It looks like you *will* be found dead in this old house after all." It was the last coherent thought Tommy Mahoney ever had before his consciousness drifted away and joined with the universe. Once again, the tired old house was filled with silence. In the basement, something waited.

THE BOOK OF I                    BY BRIAN GATTI

*May 11th, 2019*

*David,*

*I got your message about the case of Amelia Bronwyn, 27F. It took some time to compile it all.*

*You were right; this needs further action on our part.*

*Let me know what you want me to do.*

*Sincerely, Thomas*

*Field Director - North American Ops*

Encl:
Journal (2/9/19 - 3/30/19)
Grosse Pointe Tribune clipping (4/7/19)
Police report (4/4/19) (excerpts)
Hospital records (3/9/19 & 3/12/19) (excerpts)
TH Case summary & recommendations (5/11/19)

Cc:
KM, Records
JT, Enforcement

# Exhibit A - Journal

February 9th, 2019

*I* have never been much for journaling, but my doctor thinks it would be good for me to do it. She said by writing my experiences down, I can keep a grasp on objective reality.

Whatever that means.

I am the head of early childhood development at Grosse Pointe Academy. I always wanted to work with young kids.

My two loving parents are currently traveling the world on a well-earned retirement vacation.

Life was simple. Dating. Working. Small local trips. Not exactly Sex and the City, but it was good for me.

Then everything went to hell.

I remember it starting with the Book of Letters series. I was at the library looking for inspiration for class content. One of the librarians recommended them to me.

Kids' books written for the 3 to 6 age range. Each book takes a letter and wraps a story around it, using each letter in a sentence. There are millions of books out there like it.

I found a complete set on eBay for $20, which might not sound like a big deal, but it was almost impossible to find. All the sets I'd seen were incomplete and missing the Book of I.

It was only a Tuesday afternoon purchase. Nothing special.

When they came, they were great. Each was colorful and well cared for. Vintage-looking, the series was published in the early 1920s. The art was sort of abstract, but the images were friendly and appealing.

I didn't realize something was weird until I set them all up on my office shelf. Sitting in the ninth spot was the Book of I. Unlike the others, the colors were faded, and the spine's lettering was skewed as though misprinted. It stood out like an infected tooth in a mouth full of white teeth.

Already by writing this, it is giving me anxiety. I need a break.

Did I remember to turn the stove off? Shit. I should check.

February 13, 2019

Sorry for taking so long to come back to this. Dr. Ni told me I needed to get back to this to help me.

I met Dr. Wojian Ni when my parents arranged for me to get help with everything going on. I didn't want to, but they wanted me to see someone who could help me process everything. She insisted I stay focused on my treatment, and that writing down what happened is important.

The kids were enjoying the book of letters materials, and I was able to create all kinds of activities. I started with making puppets based on the characters. It was cute and harmless. Right?

However, I'll admit I felt an odd sense of revulsion when I opened the Book of I. It's the best way to describe it. Like a visceral sense of something disgusting, but it felt so irrational I disregarded it.

I wish I hadn't.

Like all the books, the first page introduced us to the characters. This one was Izzy. Usually, the characters were normal kids with a surprising diversity, considering the age of the publication.

But Izzy was different. She had a pale face with black scribbles for eyes and mouth. Her hair was a chaotic swirl of black that wrapped around her body.

The next page showed Izzy in front of a house with the words, "I see you."

It creeped me out!

I have to stop now and run some errands. Need to get gas for the car, and I should get it checked. It must have a leak.

February 14, 2019

Every time I think of the book, I feel like Izzy is getting closer to me. I told Dr. Ni it is as if she's staring at me everywhere I go.

I first confessed my feelings about it to my best friend Ti. She's the third-grade art teacher at the school. The kids call her Ms. Vedo. She was a good friend, but she didn't take me seriously. I guess, I wouldn't either.

I tried to stop thinking about it but kept seeing her face.

I looked in the mirror for the first time today in weeks. She was there! A drawing on the wall behind me. Watching me. Seeing me! When I turned around, there was nothing.

I don't even know where the book is anymore. I wish she'd leave me alone now.

I need to focus.

Hold on, there's someone at the door. It must be the guy from the gas company. I've been smelling something weird in the house.

Ok, back. No one was there, probably the neighborhood kids.

The rest of the Book of I is so strange. Despite my feeling of fear, I went back to it. Compelled.

Page 3 has Izzy in front of the same house but closer. You could see a window in the front with Izzy saying, "I see you."

Page 4 shows a woman in the window reading a book. Izzy is looking in the window, again with the words, "I see you." above the illustration.

Did you know the book was published on September 3rd, 1921? This illustrator was not the same as the other books. It was the only one with a different artist, Yatebya Vizhu.

I looked her up. Yatebya was an immigrant who fled the Russian Revolution. Unsurprisingly, there was little detail about her life. Only learned that her art made for some unknown reason made her a target of those in power. She committed suicide shortly after the Book of I was published.

*I wasn't surprised when I read that, and I'm still unsure why.*

March 9th, 2019

*Even being in the hospital is no escape for me.*

*We had an ice storm a few weeks ago. The roads were icy. You must be careful with Michigan roads when it's bad, but I was distracted. I thought I saw her black scribble eyes in my rearview mirror, watching me.*

*I was only distracted for a moment, but it was enough. I took the turn too fast and spun out, hitting a tree.*

*I woke up in the ICU.*

*The hospital doctor said I was lucky. I was unconscious for a week. During that time, they couldn't reach my parents. They were out of contact on vacation on the island of 'Arak. My only other emergency contact was Dr. Ni.*

*My life is pathetic.*

*Dr. Ni brought me my journal, so here I am writing.*

Page 5 of the Book of I showed the woman clearly. I thought she kind of looked like me. Izzy was at the door saying, as always, "I see you."

This is getting to me. Ok, push through.

Dr. Ni said my thoughts of the woman looking like me are understandable. We subconsciously frame the unfamiliar with familiar contexts.

I think she's full of shit, but what do I know? I'm the crazy one.

Page 6 showed the inside of the house with Izzy next to the woman. I have a mole on my right cheek. The woman did, too. Dr Ni said I'm looking for validation of my delusions. I think it's me. As always, Izzy says, "I see you."

Last night, I saw Izzy in my dreams. She was screaming without sound, staring at me with her scribble eyes!

Page 7 showed me getting ready for bed. The woman, not me. Not me. Right? Of course, not me. And Izzy was in my bed waiting.

I see you.

March 21st, 2019

Yesterday was a pretty terrible fucking day.

The day started simply enough. I'd been back to school for about a week. The kids were so sweet and supportive. I dropped the whole letter book idea and switched to some materials I'd done earlier in the school year. I'd been feeling kind of normal, and the meds Dr. Ni put me on seemed to be helping. I hadn't seen Izzy that whole time.

Two nights ago, I lost my new meds. They abruptly vanished and went missing. I called Ni for more, but she was out of the office. I had to go without.

So yesterday. Let's talk about yesterday.

I freaked out. I was doing a storybook with my kids when I spotted Izzy sitting in the circle with them. Her hair stretched out to cover the kids, revealing her naked body. It was covered in scratches and cuts. She looked like someone had thrown the drawing through a window.

None of the kids saw her, but I did! Taunting me. Seeing me. I started screaming. The kids were terrified. The police were called. No charges were filed, but I was fired.

Thankfully, Dr. Ni agreed to keep helping me without insurance. Ti helped me pay for some things so I didn't lose my house, but I could tell she was done with me and my crazy.

Dr. Ni was able to help me get a hold of my parents, as they were in a place where they could be contacted. I didn't speak to them directly. I had been sedated for a while, but he explained everything. They sent me money. I could pay Dr. Ni my bills and repay Ti for all the cash she'd been lending me since my accident.

I used the new payment app, Teveo, to pay her back. It was the last time she spoke to me. I miss her.

It's cold in here. The heat isn't working. Did I pay the gas bill?

Ok. Pushing through. Almost done, I think.

Page 8 showed the woman in a car, driving with Izzy in the back. They were in an old-style car, a black model T. It was snowy outside, and Izzy's scribble eyes were in the mirror. The page said, "I see you."

Of course, you do, you psycho bitch! Fuck Izzy. Fuck her to hell. Fuck!!!

The goddamn book predicted my accident. Dr. Ni said it was a coincidence. I wish I could find the book to show her, to prove it.

Page 9 showed the hospital with me lying in bed. Instead of tubes and wires attached to the woman, it was Izzy's hair. Invading her body. Invading MY body.

I see you.

*It makes my skin crawl. I can feel her hair in my brain. Her scribble eyes were staring at me.*

## March 21, 2019

*Oh, what a hell I'm in.*

*Dr. Ni said my parents called her. They're worried about me and having travel issues trying to get home. Their plane had some kind of fuel leak. She gave them an update about me, that I'm getting better. I'm not, but she said it was the right thing to tell them.*

*Why worry them needlessly?*

*We even recorded a video of me to send to them.*

*Dr. Ni is pushing me to finish recording my experiences. I just want to be done. She said I almost am, and it'll be so freeing to put it all down on paper. I'll be able to get my life back.*

*I hope so.*

*I'd like to see the kids again. I know I can't. The academy was very clear. I'm never to return. I miss the kids. They were my family.*

*I know it's pathetic. So what? I loved them.*

*I'm so lonely. It's just me and Dr Ni and my imaginary tormentor.*

*I see you.*

*I tried calling Ti to say sorry and explain, but her line was disconnected. Just the dead robot voice, "Your call cannot be completed as dialed, error code 9321."*

*I get it. I'd abandon me, too.*

*Page 9 showed the woman sitting in a chair with Izzy behind her. Izzy's hair was wrapped tight around the woman's face. Smothering her. It must've been hard to breathe. And, of course, the words...*

*I see you. I see you. I see you!!*

*Ik zie je. Anata ga mietemasu.*

*I wish I could find the book. I don't know where it went. It's not in my box of stuff from the school. I'd fucking burn it and laugh.*

*I hope Yatebya Vizhu is in hell for drawing, that soulless bitch.*

*Dr. Ni says this aggression I'm feeling is a manifestation of my feelings of unworthiness and self-loathing. I miss my parents. I wish they weren't gone. It's been so long. Why did they have to leave?*

*Sometimes, I feel it's my fault they left, but that's ridiculous.*

I take pills to sleep. Sometimes, it keeps me from seeing Izzy and her eyes. It keeps her from seeing me. Those nights of emptiness are the best. Just peace.

March 30, 2019

Underneath it all, I can't say I'm surprised.

Dr. Ni got a call. My parents' flight back is delayed again. They're never coming home, I think.

Their disappointment in me is too much. What else could it be?

I'm twenty-seven with no job, husband, or kids. I'm just their crazy daughter. Thankfully, they are still helping me financially, but it's not enough. The power may be off at my house.

The nights are so cold, but I have a fireplace which helps. I've had to take to burning some furniture to keep warm.

Dr. Ni says that I'm alright this way. I shouldn't be scared.

I don't think I am scared anymore.

I remembered the last page of the book last night. It was a weird sort of dream. Izzy was there along with Dr. Ni, Ti, and my parents. Her hair was wrapped around everyone. They left a place in the middle for me.

Strangely, I didn't feel so alone anymore. It felt more like being with those who loved me.

I woke up crying.

Page 10 showed a woman in an empty, broken-looking house. The woman looked as broken and filthy as the home. Izzy stood nearby with her hair twisted into the letter O.

I see you, said the page.

I see you too, Izzy.

I'm going to call Dr. Ni today and let her know I've figured it out. I'm better now.

**I SEE YOU.**

## Exhibit B - Grosse Pointe Tribune, April 7, 2019

### Woman Found Dead in Family Home

Amelia Bronwyn, aged twenty-seven, was found dead of apparent suicide in the abandoned home of her parents, Stephen and Linda Bronwyn.

The Grosse Pointe PD conducted a routine wellness visit to the reclusive woman. A lack of response at the door prompted the officers to enter, and her body was discovered.

Stephen and Linda died on September 3rd, 2018, when a gas leak from the stove asphyxiated them. Their daughter, Amelia, lived in the home and worked as a teacher at Grosse Pointe Academy until parent complaints resulted in her termination.

Amelia moved into her parents' home shortly after their deaths, sustained by a small inheritance left to her by her parents.

People who knew her remarked that Amelia became withdrawn and increasingly paranoid after her parents died. She was briefly hospitalized for an accident but left before discharge.

Services will be held at Grosse Pointe Methodist Church. Donations in place of flowers should be sent to the American Society for Suicide Prevention.

## Exhibit C - Police Report (4/4/19) (Excerpted)

Officers Jacobs & Villay

```
Routine Wellness Check
```

0903

> Knocked at the door three times. Jacobs walked the exterior of the home. No broken windows. No signs of activity. Mail piled in the mailbox.
>
> Knocked on the side dining window and back door. No response.
>
> Called dispatch and received permission to use the vacation key.

0907

> Opened the rear door to the kitchen. The house was dark, and a strong stench came out.
>
> Garbage was scattered on the floor. It appeared as though the room had been intentionally damaged. We called out and received no response.
>
> Moved to the dining room. More trash. House was very cold. Likely the heat had not been on for a while.
>
> Creepy drawings on the wall of people with scribbled-out eyes and mouths.

Above the drawings was written in large letters, *I see you.*

[Black and white photo included - The dining room is cluttered with trash. A fireplace is visible in the living room to the right. The drawings cover the walls, looking as though a child did them. A large decorative mirror on the wall has been shattered.]

0910

Upstairs, we found Amelia hanging from a ceiling beam. The black rope was strange, maybe nylon? Looked like thickly braided hair.

She was dead. She looked thin, and her pale body was covered in cuts and scrapes.

[Black and white photo included - Amelia's body was hanging limply from the hairlike rope. Her naked skin was visible through her long hair. Pale flesh was torn as though by broken glass. Wounds showed signs of infection.]

# Exhibit D - Hospital records (3/9/19 & 3/12/19) (excepts)

## 3/9/19

Patient was admitted after an accident. She was unconscious, and there was no identification with her. A note in her pocket indicated she was under the care of a psychiatrist, Dr. Wojian Ni.

We could not find anyone with this name licensed to practice medicine in Michigan.

Examination of the patient revealed trauma to the head and superficial cuts on her face and arms due to the accident.

Patient appeared to be undernourished, and her body was covered in wounds, many of which were old and poorly healed.

Recommend psychiatric evaluation for DTS and possible commitment to long-term care.

Patient says her name is Isabelle.

## 3/12/19

Patient left the hospital AMA and without release. Police were called and a description was provided.

Exhibit E - TH Case summary & recommendations (5/11/19)

## Summary:

*Amelia was wracked with guilt over her parents' deaths, and the grief became unmanageable.*

*Amelia was terminated well before the date in her journal. The head of the school cited her erratic and troubling behavior.*

*Amelia acquired a legitimate copy of the Book of I. This means prior elimination efforts were ineffective, or the Book can reform. (eBay seller username is IcyEwe9321 - only one sale, likely a dead end).*

*We should raise the priority on this item as destroying it was ineffective.*

*While the risk for mass impact is low, the insidious nature of the artifact and its apparent ability to recreate itself means there is a risk of escalation.*

*The next step is to investigate the original publishing house and find the source of the Book of I.*

*Sincerely, Thomas*

*ISOLATED*                                            *BY DEREK BARTON*

**INITIAL INVESTIGATION REPORT** – 10/28/19:
Led by Sedona Police Dept in conjunction with National Forestry Service.

**ANNUAL FOLLOW-UP INVESTIGATION REPORT**— 1/15/2020:
Investigations & Interviews conducted by Detective Joseph Stouts

**ANNUAL FOLLOW-UP INVESTIGATION REPORT**— 11/7/2021:
Open Investigation led by Detective Reese Arbor

11/14/2021 –
My first step is to review the evidence found at the site. I am starting with viewing the video taken by the cell phone's owner. The video has the date and battery amount displayed in the corner.

*96% - 10/19/2019*

"God! I feel so stupid. I never would have thought I would be doing a 'found footage' video, but here I am." The man on the video spoke angrily and then scanned the surrounding rocks and empty desert landscape about him.

"Okay. Sorry. Let me start again. My name is Merritt Thomas. It's Saturday afternoon. Or is it already Monday? I kind of lost track after my fall," he paused to take a deep breath. Merritt appeared to be in athletic shape with short blonde hair, light green eyes, and pale but sun-burnt skin. Under his red rain poncho, the young man had a green Coyotes

Hockey Team beanie cap. A scabbed-over, bloody laceration ran across his forehead and partially down his left cheek.

"If you are watching this... man, that phrase sounds so weird! I mean I have seen all sorts of 'disturbing videos' on YouTube where someone begins their tale with those words, but how did I even get into this position? It's all so surreal. Anyway, if you are watching this video then that means I may not have made it out of this damn crevice." He stopped again and looked up off-camera.

"The crevice isn't that wide, five or six feet, but at least seventy feet deep. I was camping by myself which I never normally do. My best friend Marc Gordon had to bail on the trip at the last minute. It's not your fault, man. Don't even think of blaming yourself. I chose to come out here alone. Took me a lot of finagling to arrange this time off from work, so I couldn't pass this up. I wasn't going to miss this opportunity. In hindsight, I guess, it wasn't my brightest decision."

The shadows cover a lot of the area around him. A small pair of cacti grew behind him and a softly babbling stream was somewhere nearby off-screen.

"Friday night went well. I beat the rush hour traffic out of town and came north, near the Sedona region. Hiked till sundown, then made camp. It was perfect weather, no rain, clear starry skies. You'll see my collection of photos on the phone here." Birds squawked above in the distance as they flew over the crevice's opening.

"I made dinner. Caught a pair of bass actually using those new lures you got me for my birthday, Mom." He laughed, smiled, and then teared up for a second. "Mom, Dad, I love you so much. I really do! I'm sorry I didn't always make a lot of effort to show you that. I have been so focused on my work and trying to advance in the food chain at Phillips & Grant.

It's not an excuse, but I wanted you to know it was not ever my intention. I'm so sorry if I ever made you feel I didn't value all you've done for me and all the support you have given me through law school."

He wiped away a couple of streaking tears from his cheek. Then grinned again at the camera. "See, look at me! Already letting my fears get away from me. Well, not this time. I am going to find a way to get home. We can watch this dumb video and laugh at my stupid ass all together. Promise! Anyway, it's getting dark. Going to try and sleep. I'll update again in the morning. Lucky me I bought one of those battery rechargers. I should have enough energy on this phone for at least a couple more days or maybe till Wednesday if I am careful. Night."

Video stops.

### 93% -- 10/20/2019

The video started again. Nearly pitch black. The raspy sound of cloth moving could be heard, perhaps his poncho.

"I am so scared," Merritt whispered. "I don't know what it is, but I keep hearing this sound. It's like a growl, but almost as if it is a person who is doing it too. Like someone trying to howl or copy the coyotes out here. On Friday night about 2 AM or so in the morning, I think it was what woke me up originally."

He paused to listen. Except for the cadence of crickets and other nocturnal insects, there are no other noises on the video. He craned his neck to look up and scanned the surrounding rock. "Anyway, I woke up. I am not a sound sleeper, and this wasn't the best ground to camp on. Since I was awake, I decided to go take a piss. As I was coming back to the tent, I heard this howling noise. Whatever it was sent chills up my spine. It sounded big too. I sprinted back to the tent and grabbed my phone and my flashlight. If there was a bear or a wolf around, I wanted to scare it off. Didn't want to get a surprise later when I slept, you know."

Merritt brought the phone around and spoke again to the camera. "I waited to hear the howl once more. When I did, it was further down the trail than before. I ran. I guess I needed to see it. That's when I could make out these voices. Male voices. Somewhere camping north of me. Two people having a conversation. One had a deeper tone and sounded older than the other which could have been a male child. I couldn't make out the whole conversation, but just some words. I think they were in English. After fifteen minutes of looking for the Howler or maybe the two other campers, I decided to quit and turn back. It was getting cold. On the way back, I stumbled over a root and dropped the flashlight. I didn't know where it went. It must've bounced then shut off or rolled a bit down the slope into this crevice."

He stopped, shivered, and wiped beads of water from his forehead. "Crap! Starting to rain again. It's been on and off since yesterday morning. Well, at least from when I woke up from the fall. Yeah," he laughed and shook his head in seeming disbelief. "I made the classic, 'Big No-no mistake'. Went off trail looking for the flashlight in the dark and like an idiot walked right off the edge and fell down here."

He cleared his throat. "I want to warn you before I turn the camera around to show you the result. This isn't pretty. Uh, Mom, look away!"

The camera shifted and a sudden flash of light showed his legs and feet. His left leg was angled madly off to the side, obviously broken. On the other foot was a blood-splattered white sneaker. A belt was cinched tightly above the ankle on his calf. "Broke both of my legs. Snapped the bone out above the ankle here."

He then panned the camera showing the small muddy bank of a stream with deep russet-orange rocks and boulders. Sparse river grass and more cacti made up the majority of the landscape.

Above him, off-camera, a horrid grunting and growling howl echoed all about the crevice. The flashlight clicked off. He angled the camera to focus on the bit of sky shown above. It was night, but dark gray clouds blotted the limited light. Nothing appeared to move, and no other sounds were repeated. The night crickets had stopped. Merritt stopped the video.

**90% -- 10/21/2019**

"I am not sure I captured that sound, the howling, or not on video. I don't want to waste power trying to find out by reviewing."

It was morning, sunlight lit up the rocky background behind him. His hair was greasy and stuck up on one side. He looked haggard and exhausted. Most likely he hadn't slept since the last part of the video.

"It stopped raining a few minutes ago. May even be sunny up there but it's not getting much in here. The Howler went away after about an hour. It could've been hunting this small pack of coyotes I saw the other day on my hike. Not sure—," he stopped as a spasm of coughing caught him by surprise.

"Well...that's a bad sign. I might have the flu or worse starting. If this is Monday, then some people at work should notice I'm out or maybe Marc might be wondering why he can't reach me by now. Either way, I'm looking at another long day and night in here or even two days. I'm in the elements for sure but not out under the sky completely."

He paused, rubbed at his stubbly chin with a pained expression, then looked at the camera. "I'm soaked from head-to-toe by the rain and yet I'm severely dehydrated." He chuckled weakly.

Merritt rotated the camera around to video the length of the crevice. The small stream ran about a dozen feet from him and cut through the cliff rock. "I am going to try and crawl over there. I want a sip of that stream so badly!"

The camera flipped back toward him. "Should I keep the recording going? Do you want to witness the greatest endurance test I've ever taken? Or... No. On second thought, I might do some serious screaming and using some choice words that would upset Mom." Another half-hearted attempt at humor.

The video stopped.

**82% -- 10/21/2019**

Merritt faced the camera again. His condition looked more haggard and with thicker stubble. Mud smeared down one side of his head to the base of his shoulder. His jacket had been torn. The green beanie was also missing.

"It is right after sundown. The good news is I got to the stream, drank some, and even managed to find an old water bottle to drink from later. The water tastes terrible, but it's cool and probably filled with every known variant of parasites in existence." He sneezed hard. Sneezed again and once more. He then trembled. "That's part of the bad news. I dragged myself through the mud bank by arm strength alone. Hurt so bad! Never would have thought pain could get that intense, but I battled through it. I had to take the rest of the day though to recover. My right leg is getting, uh, what they call Compartment Syndrome."

Merritt shook his head. A frustrated and pained expression crossed his face. "I have to get help soon! The Syndrome causes swelling under the wall of muscle due to the extreme injury. Basically, blood is welling up, cutting off the oxygen in the leg. Muscles and nerves will die permanently. I may never walk again!"

He stopped, coughed, and choked up with emotion.

"Sorry. Can't right –" He reached for the phone and the video ended again.

**73% -- 10/22/2019**

The video restarted but there wasn't any image. Again, it was pitch dark, but the water still babbled in the background.

A pair of pale orange, almost red eyes opened. They were not near but seemed above Merritt's position. A soft purring echoed down the cliff walls. It was a striking, odd noise, not cat-like as from a lynx or cougar. It had a whining pitch that paired with the purring cadence.

The purring ended and a voice spoke out from above. It was hollow, monotone, and somewhat slurred. The voice was very similar to Merritt's.

"Sysssdrrrum caws mussel swallin...sssdrem cacawsez mussel swelling... ssyndome cause muscle swelling –" The words cut off as a coyote howl pierced the night. A pair of other coyotes joined in chorus with the first.

"Syndrome causes muscle swellling do-due to the exxksteen..." The words continued as the pair of orange-red eyes moved closer.

"He-heello? Hi?" The voice asked aloud in the dark.

Merritt didn't answer or couldn't.

"Hi? Help you?"

Still no response or movement.

There was a rustling in the brush at the top of the opening. A pair of lupine growls could be heard. The coyote pack was hunting at the top.

After a loud sigh and a yawn, the glowing orbs ascended back up the rock walls. At the ledge, a flash of ivory skin was caught on the video. It was fast and blurred, but it proved that Merritt had definitely not been alone in the crevice.

The video stopped again. The battery had slipped to 59%.

**46% -- 10/22/2019**

"I might be delusional, but I think someone was calling my name. I was in and out of sleep all night." It was daylight and Merritt was recording another entry. His eyes were red-rimmed and swollen. His left eye was completely red from a broken blood vessel.

"At least it sounded like my name. And it sounded like a real person. Was that a rescue party?" he wondered aloud. "Not sure what that was last night." He brought the camera close and whispered intimately. "I mean that happened right? Or was that a hallucination? Did I only record the night air, or did you guys hear that voice too?"

His voice sounded gravelly, thick, and strained. His eyes had large dark patches under them. His hair stuck out at the sides and his lips were scanned with sores.

"I don't...I don't think I am going to make it much longer. If they don't find me before dark—," his words were chopped short by a series of harsh coughs rattling deep inside his chest. He grabbed the phone and ended the video again.

**28% -- 10/23/2019**

"Hi? Hello? Merritt?"

It was that monotone voice again only slightly more animated, clearer, and sounded even closer to his voice more than ever.

"Yes. Yes, I'm here. Thank God, you found me!" Merritt cried out. His words were barely audible on the recording. Night had fallen in the desert.

"You need help? Where are you?" it asked.

"By the water."

"Who were you talking to?"

Merritt laughed at the question. "No one. I'm alone with just my cellphone."

"Stay there. Do not...worry... I'll help you."

"I'll turn on the flash so you can see your way down better."

The flash of his phone blazed to life. Looming above his prone body was a long, lanky creature. It had a snakelike body with twin legs and clawed arms protruding and gripping the stone walls. The head was elongated with spikey, blonde hair and tan skin. The face was striking similar to Merritt's!

When the brilliance hit its almond-shaped, green eyes, it screeched and lashed out with a set of elongated fingers. The camera bounced wildly and then splashed into a puddle of mud. The flash was buried but the camera kept recording.

Merritt began to scream and thrash as the creature fell upon him.

"Stop! I help you! Stop moving! Must have you! I am help!"

Merritt's blood-curdling screams suddenly stopped. A gurgling sound could be heard over the stream's noises.

A few moments of silence followed.

"Merritt. My name is Merritt. I...I was camping." The voice was muffled as if the mouth were full. "I fell, but I am okay now. Don't worry Mom. Don't worry or look for Merr-me. I'm fine. Going on vacation. Come home soon."

The video stopped.

The Video Tech clerks surmised it ran out of battery.

## FINDINGS & SUMMARY:

Merritt Thomas is still missing. His raincoat, boots, tent, and of course his phone were all eventually located.

It is not clear if Merritt had fallen victim to foul play or if this is a very complex hoax perpetrated for the Internet. Some speculate he had faked this to avoid a possible gambling debt but no evidence to that claim has ever been found. Due to remarks made in the video, in my professional opinion, I am inclined to think this is an elaborate setup to gain some recognition or attention. Merritt had a busy Instagram account and a propensity for pranks per friends and family interviewed. However, no financial transaction or credit card activity has been reported since his disappearance. The family insists that this is not within Mr. Thomas's character, and he had a great bond with his young sister and parents.

To date, with no remains or body ever found, thus the case must remain open.

*Addendum –

2/19/2022: WITNESS SIGHTING REPORT

On 2/11/2022 a married couple while hiking a trail in the northern tip of Fishlake National Forest in Utah, claimed they saw Merritt Thomas. A white man, in his mid-twenties matching his description, approached them. They stated they recognized him as they had been living in Phoenix, Arizona, at the time when Thomas was first reported missing in the news. Upon speaking briefly with the couple, the male subject left the trail and went deeper into the forest without any further response. He did not have any backpack or camping gear with him.

# 4/23/2023 WITNESS SIGHTING REPORT

During the evening of 4/15/2023, three men were attacked and severely beaten by a white male in his mid-twenties. When the men entered a cave to go spelunking in Spring Cave Park near Buford, Colorado, the man ambushed them. Police investigated the cave site and only found animal remains. One worn-out ID bracelet with the only readable letters as M...I..T was collected. Days later, one of the victims came across an image of Merritt Thomas posted on a Missing Persons' website and identified him as the individual who attacked them.

Detective Reese Arbor

THE CYCLE                    BY DEREK BARTON


I extended my arms upward in a languid stretch and yawned. My security guard uniform pulled tight across my shoulders. It was as worn out as I was. Especially since I had to cover another twelve-hour shift directly coming from my second job at Home Depot. It was destined to be a long night.

I had no idea it would be the longest one of my life.

The bank of television screens mounted on the wall showed nine camera angles. The views were mostly of an empty parking lot. The room lights were dimmed and smoke from my partner's cigarette drifted high toward the ceiling. I snapped a glance at the clock. 8:28 PM. Parkerson Mills Mall was closing in almost a half hour. There were only a few shoppers left to roam about.

"Tom," I called out over my shoulder. "I'm going across the hall real quick to hit the john, then I'll do a patrol on the southside, okay?"

I got only a grunt back in response. Tom Dawson was not the talkative type. He was, however, a heavyset man with a salt-and-pepper receding hairline. A set of luggage-sized bags under his eyes matched his second and third chin. His eyes remained glued to the monitor in front of him. It was his job to watch the alarm program for all the door badge readers.

After snatching a long-handle flashlight resting on the desk, I walked out.

Our office was tucked away in an obscure corridor of the mall's eastern wing, an almost forgotten nook. The air was stale, musty from dirty mop water, and humid as the AC's temperature was kept on high to save money. Only steps away, a glass door marked the bathroom entrances.

I pushed past the glass door and stepped to the right into the men's bathroom. After I did my business, I rinsed my hands and splashed a healthy amount of water onto my face. I studied the rough stubble on my unshaven cheeks. Then I smoothed down a dark blonde duck tail sticking out over my white collar. With disdain, I noted my own small set of luggage forming under my blue eyes.

"Getting uglier and older every day, my man," I muttered to myself.

The stall door behind me swung open with a clatter as a tall, white man stepped out. He was dressed in an expensive black suit and a white button-down shirt with a flat blue tie.

"Aging's a heartless bitch, ain't she?" he said with a glint of dark humor in his sharp, gray eyes.

I laughed but was startled by the man's sudden appearance. "Yes. Yes." I replied.

I bent down again to splash my face one more time with water when I sensed rather than felt the man sidestep behind me.

"What—"

Thick, clear plastic swept down over my face, awkwardly pinning some of my fingers to my chin. The plastic stretched tight across my mouth and nose. I immediately could not breathe!

I gasped, choked, and gagged in reflex. I was caught in the guy's vice-like embrace. I swung my right arm in wild arches trying to break free. At that same moment, my eyes locked on the fuzzy image of my attacker in the mirrors above the row of sinks. The man's features were unclear, but a large, toothy smile was spread across his face. It was sharklike, almost crystal clear. A true predator's grin!

I slapped and then scratched at the plastic wrapping, fighting to make holes to breathe through. My struggles soon faded as my vision tunneled away into a black murky inkiness.

As I collapsed on the greasy bathroom floor, I heard deep chuckles followed by a "That's a good boy!".

\* \* \* \*

"...a good boy!"

I jumped awake, tilted back in a padded passenger seat. A car door opened outside next to me as an old woman climbed into her rusting, gold Ford Crown Victoria. "Good boy, Geoffie! Waitin' on Mama. Such a good boy!" she called cheerfully to her small blonde chihuahua. It was bouncing up and down in the seat to greet her.

Another door opened on my left and I jumped again nearly out of my skin.

"Hey, dude, you should get one of these. They're only half the cost today!" It was Chris Gatti, my best friend, now ongoing for nine years. He's younger than me with cropped brown hair, dressed in a green hoodie and jeans. He plopped down, sipping on a large fountain drink.

Despite being a few years younger, he possessed an old soul with a very generous nature. "I'm serious—" Chris said, then stopped when he saw the terrified expression on my face. "Whoa. What's wrong?"

I couldn't answer. My mind was still absorbing the traumatic attack moments before.

*How? What just happened? Why am I here?*

A tempest of questions stormed through my head.

Hot rays of sunlight poured in through the windshield. I could see the skies were the bright, crystalline blue of summer. But that did not make any sense either. I was working the night shift.

"Did you have a nightmare or something?"

"I... uh, a nightmare?" I mumbled, completely at a loss for words. A nightmare, though, did strike me as a plausible answer to the craziness of the assault. After all, why would anyone attack me? I hadn't done anything to anyone, and no one had any beefs with me that I could recall. And I didn't recognize the strange man who jumped me at Parkerson's.

"Yeah, you were snoozing like a baby when I pulled in for gas. I didn't wanna wake you when I went in."

I nodded. The confusion and odd sense of Deja-vu unnerved me. "Yeah, probably just a bad dream." But it didn't feel like any dream. Nothing ever felt so real!

"Tell me, man. Musta been a doozy," Chris asked as he started his Kia Soul.

"Don't remember much. Hey, hold up. Do you mind if I do get a drink after all?" I asked, wanting to escape having to tell the story and relive the ambush.

"Sure thing."

\* \* \* \*

Inside the gas station store, the frigid air thoroughly chilled me. My clothes were damp from sweat and my exposed skin was goose bumped. I pulled down the rolled-up sleeves of my Tampa Bay Buccaneers sweatshirt on my arms and headed for the back. The place was cramped with close rows and displays blocking the entrances. A young teenage couple walked past me holding hands, giggling, and lost in their private world of puppy love. Other than the short, Italian man at the register singing along to an old rock tune on the radio, all was quiet.

The lights were amazingly bright. The glare made me squint. The multitude of items on the shelves were ablaze with neon firework colors. I never got migraines, but I once heard that people suffering from them had similar, intense reactions to light. I shook my head, but it didn't clear up my vision.

I kept my face pointed at my shoes and walked briskly to the soda fountains. My throat was sore from the strangulation! It was tender to the touch along the sides. I remembered screaming and gasping for air...

I stretched over the counter for one of the large size foam cups stacked beside the fountain machines.

Tight, clear plastic dropped down over my face again, cutting off my air, and dimming the light.

"NO!!" I shrieked.

My words – my plea – came out muffled and muted. I wasted no time. I swung around with my arms spread wide and my fingers clawing the air. I wanted to get my hands on this bastard. Beat the man back, kick the man in revenge, and smash my attacker into the ground forever!

In my efforts, my arms knocked over a potato chip rack and my hands sent a coffee pot to a shattering end upon the tiled floor.

The young teen girl squeaked in surprise at the register.

"What's going on back there? You will pay for anything you've broken! I swear it to God!" the clerk exclaimed.

Thinking I might break the stranger's hold, I coiled my legs and propelled them backward. I was hoping to drive him against a counter or one of the nearby freezers. Instead, we plowed into a glass donut enclosure. There was another tinkling explosion of broken glass. It fell next to where we continued to wrestle.

My sight again darkened as a chilling numbness spread over me.

*Why is this happening? Who is he? What the fuck does he waaaa...*

More deep chuckles followed me into the gloom.

\* \* \* \*

"Yo! Are you next? Ya waiting on somethin' or is the machine down, man?" Someone was upset behind me.

I blinked and wavered on my feet. The world shifted up and down.

As it settled, a pair of strong hands gripped my shoulders. "Hey man, you okay?"

Once more, I could not answer and looked into the face of an elderly black man. He must have come up behind me through a glass door marked CHANNEL BANK - ATM.

"What?" I mumbled. My body was numb. He was still holding me upright.

"I asked if you were alright?" Concern creased his wrinkled features. His dark eyes implored and studied my face.

"Honestly, I don't know."

I shrugged free of the man and left the small ATM enclosure without another word. Outside it was cloudy and sprinkling. A heavily loaded Metro bus grunted and then hissed as it progressed down Main Street. Its brakes whined in protest as it slowed to make its turn down 5th Avenue. I shuffled toward an old park bench near the curb facing the street.

I plopped down, planted my face in my hands, and leaned over my grubby sneakers. It was too much. The pain, the terror, the icy sensation coming over me each time at the end. The trauma was overwhelming. The terror and the pain carried over from the nightmares. I couldn't stop myself and I sobbed helplessly in my palms.

Moments later, I finally gathered myself and straightened my shoulders, leaning back.

*This is like some cheesy horror movie! Only I'm the one that Michael or Freddie keeps going after.*

Like in those movies, that my friends and I saw in my teenage years, I realized I needed to find answers. Needed to research how and why this kept happening. Yet, those answers were most likely only found on the net. I wasn't going to dare go home to my empty apartment, to my laptop. Hell, I never wanted to be alone anywhere again!

I remembered there were public laptops at the city center library. I waited on edge for the next bus which would come and get me close to downtown. The traffic and the few pedestrians on the sidewalk kept me company. I was deeply grateful for that.

\* \* \* \*

The cursor kept blinking and waiting for my search keywords.

*What do I look for? Do I try to find out who that man is? Do I see if anyone else has been attacked recently?*

I stared at the laptop screen in frustration. Half a dozen other users were sitting at the bank of laptops. Others walked among the bookshelves or browsed the magazine racks. I had never felt so happy to see a crowd. I would have gladly hugged and embraced each person. Tears rimmed my eyes again and threatened to spill down. My emotions were all over the place. I realized just how desperate I was. I was near panic mode.

I fought my emotions and got down to business. I typed "Muggings+white+40s male+plastic bag". My fingers trembled so badly that I clasped my hands together in my lap as I waited for the search results.

Several stories appeared but nothing that seemed related to what I was going through.

"C'mon! I know this guy's done this before. He's too quick, too practiced for this to be his first rodeo," I said aloud.

I needed to be broader and more general. "Strangulations+white male"

More articles but nothing specific enough to help.

"Self-defense tactics" I typed next.

A loud siren, shrieking overhead and down the hallway exits startled me so badly that I yelped. Some laughter at my reaction was quickly drowned out by a PA announcement. "EVERYONE, PLEASE EXIT THE BUILDING IN AN ORDERLY MANNER. THE FIRE ALARM IS REAL. THIS IS NOT A DRILL."

As everyone gathered their books, backpacks, and purses, the announcement was repeated.

I sighed but wasn't too upset as I was getting nowhere fast on the internet. As I followed the nervous crowd marching along the hallway, I was trying to decide what would be my next move.

*Where can I go to get answers? Where will there be a crowd? Who might understand what's happening? Would a church or a priest have some insight?*

Hands clasped my left arm and yanked me hard into an unlit meeting room as I passed by. I stumbled blindly over a chair and fell hard onto my stomach. My right wrist popped like a gunshot in the interior of the tiny room.

Through gritted teeth, I screamed as the stranger landed on top of my back, "WHY DO YOU KEEP ATTACKING ME? WHY DO YOU WANT TO KILL ME?" Hot pain seared through my arm and broken wrist.

The man's weight constricted my breathing and movements. Even over the continuous bleating of the fire alarm, I could hear the stranger's deep chuckles.

"Why do you say I'm *trying* to kill you?" More mocking laughter followed. "That's funny! I'm not trying. I AM KILLING YOU! And I'm going to kill you again and again!"

I stopped my struggles and froze in response to the words.

He then leaned in close to my left ear. "You see, Jason, you've made a very powerful enemy. Seen something or done something you weren't supposed to. I don't know. They don't pay me to know. They pay me a lot of money to not stop. I will wipe you out of existence. *Every* existence... *Every* lifetime... *Every* dimension..."

Plastic wrapped over my face again. I couldn't fight him with one arm made useless.

I was paralyzed by his words. As my vision winked out, I grasped the meaning of those words. The assassin was snuffing me out one by one. I witnessed and experienced it every time. Different versions of me from countless dimensions.

*I realized that my murder would be infinite.*

TENTH                                BY DEREK BARTON

10/28/19 – The Day Of

"When do I get tippy toes?" Mattie asked from the backseat as they pulled into the parking lot of Graham Park.

"Oh! I want some! Me too. Me too," cried his five-year-old sister, Lilly.

From behind her SUV steering wheel, Kelli muttered, "What are you talking about, little guy?"

"I heard on TV, the man said, you can reach the box on the top shelf if you stand on your tippy toes. I am ten now. I want my tippy toes. I'm grown-up and deserve to have them!" Mattie said proudly, puffing his chest out. The day before was his tenth birthday. His mother, Melissa Brandon had thrown an early Halloween/Birthday party for him and all his little classmates.

Kelli Jarvis, his exasperated nanny barely into her nineteenth year, was exhausted. She had assisted with the party and the late-hour clean-up. "That's not how it works. It's only a saying."

"No," insisted Lilly, shaking her head. "Mattie is right. We deserve tippies!" She began to drum her hands upon the armrests of her child seat.

"Yeah! We want tippies!" he laughed and chanted with her.

"Settle down, now. Or we can just go home," Kelli grumbled.

The siblings dropped the matter immediately. They had been dying to go to the park all day. It had been drizzling and they had been stuck inside, festering with "Bore-dumb Syndrome".

The public park was decked out with slides, twin rows of swings and several wooden obstacle structures to play tag around.

They scrambled out of the car and bolted away in a frenzy. Kelli glanced at her phone for the fifteenth time. Jessie still wasn't answering her texts. She opened up her door and followed the kids into the busy park.

Since the sun was shining for the first time that Saturday, many families were out including two family birthday parties.

Kelli removed her jacket. She tied it around her waist and sat down near the yellow slides. Mattie left his sister and found an empty swing.

Lilly was decked out in a baggy, red onesie. She was still chubby with baby fat and waddled slightly like a duck. Kelli couldn't help but grin at the cute toddler. Lilly spied her looking at her and waved from the top of the slide.

Her phone buzzed. It was a text.

```
No. I am going with Brett to the Derby at the
Lewiston Fair. Stop asking. I told you this.
```

Jessie could be so rude. It was their six-month anniversary after all!

Before she could respond, Lilly's scream cut through the air. The little girl was on her stomach and blood was oozing out from a swollen lip.

Kelli rushed over to assist the wailing child.

Mattie left the swings unnoticed and walked alone into the Men's Restroom.

\*\*\*

First, Kelli strolled about, scanning the park. Then, ten minutes later, she began calling his name. Her voice was strained and catching people's attention. Then she was frantic, dragging a sobbing Lilly behind her as she screamed for Mattie. Other parents by this time joined in the search. Matthew Joshua Brandon was nowhere.

"I am sorry, sweetie, it's time. You must call his mother. She deserves to know. The police are on the way." One middle-aged mother advised her.

More than an hour had already passed.

\*\*\*

A slender, athletic man walked across the park, holding a clipboard and a walkie-talkie. A gold badge adorned his shoulder. He was young with black hair and a thin baby face.

"Miss Brandon?" he asked, extending his hand. She was sitting on a bench.

She wiped tears away with the back of her hand instead of shaking his. "Yes."

"Uh... Well, I am Detective Dax Roberts, ma'am. I am lead on your son's disappearance."

"Okay," she mumbled, distracted as a roaring helicopter passed overhead. A brilliant light swept the grounds beneath it.

"We are doing everything—"

"Stop! Stop! I don't want your placating words, what you were taught to say in the academy. I just want to know you know how to bring back my little boy!" Her rant melted into a wail. She couldn't continue.

He squatted low to look into Melissa's face. He took her hands in his. "I'm sorry. I didn't mean to give the impression I wasn't engaged in this investigation or dedicated to you. I want you to know, I won't stop. I won't back off till we get Mattie back to you."

8/15/20 – Day of Discovery

Chuck and Daniel were similar in age, appearance, and even build. Good old hard-working fellas with some skills and reliable reputations as handymen. They had been hired by the city and on that morning were off in their white work pickup heading to Tandam Pond.

WXTA's news reporter droned on. His voice was void of any emotion or care. "Investigators are estimating last night's thunderstorms cost the county over $7 million in property damage. Only minor injuries were reported stemming from a collapsed construction scaffolding. The rest of the week's weather is expected to be clear."

"Sounds like we are going to be busy," Daniel said as he plugged in a county music cassette.

"Sounds good to me. That's money I can use."

"You still planning that Chicago trip?"

He nodded as he drove them to the edge of the pond. Three wooden piers had been built here but only one was untouched. Another was completely submerged. The last listing to one side with splintered boards sticking up like broken teeth.

Daniel whistled at the site.

\*\*\*

As Daniel wiggled into his plastic waders, he spotted something floating under the partial pier. It was black and two to three feet long.

"What do you think that is?" he pointed at the debris.

Chuck, who was already at the pond's edge, shrugged and made his way carefully into the pond.

The water was murky from the silt stirred up from the storm. The object was a duffle bag. Chuck noticed that one end was tied with a moss-covered nylon rope. Another piece of the rope was partially secured on the other end but rotted through.

He lifted the black bag out of the water. A sickening stench filled the air around them. Immediately, he lurched backward and thrust the bag away. He bent over and retched his breakfast into the churning water.

"Oh God! Call 911!"

\* \* \*

Detective Dax Roberts left his car. His heart was beating like a jackhammer. He saw the two handymen who had called the find in. They were noticeably shaken up. Officers were mulling around the pair.

"Detective, we haven't cut it loose yet. We can--" said a young rookie officer.

"No, I want a pro diver in there. Make sure there's nothing hidden by the water. I don't want any mistakes here." Dax waved him away.

An hour later, the diver rose from the depths of the pond, the bag held in his arms. The outline of a small body in a tight fetal position was clearly evident. A tuft of brown hair stuck out from a zipper on top. The sight would haunt his nightmares for years.

Dax didn't need DNA or an autopsy to know who was inside the bag.

10/28/29 - The Day to Remember

The detective angled his car into a spot near the main building of Humbolt Cemetery. The day was unusually hot for this time of year. Dax removed a couple of plain manilla folders from underneath his jacket on the bench seat.

He sat for a few seconds to collect his thoughts. He glanced at the rearview mirror. Quite a few wrinkles had gathered around the edges of his eyes. He had lost his babyface years ago. He rubbed at the black and gray stubble on his chin.

He asked his reflection, "She's not going to be easy on you. You must know that." He nodded to himself and shot a look at the folders on his lap. Sighing in resignation, he opened the door.

At the east side of the building, paths were laid out with white gravel. They wound their way over to different plots. He took the path that ascended a small grassy hill with some towering oaks on top. When he crested the hill and stood in the shade of the trees, he spotted Melissa Brandon in a shady section at the bottom. She faced away from him, looking down on a silvery blue headstone.

Dax ran his hand through his hair, smoothing it out as best he could. The detective didn't say anything as he joined her before Mattie's final resting place. For several minutes, they remained silent.

Finally, she said, "Thank you, Detective Roberts, for agreeing to meet me here. It's rather nice, isn't it?" She was looking up, scanning the woody area ahead of them. A short, black iron fence ran along the north side and continued along the west border of the cemetery. A lazy stream cut through diagonally and meandered further east to skirt the grassy hill.

"Yes. That it is, Miss—"

"Oh please, call me Melissa," she interrupted him.

"Okay, Melissa. You found him a very proper lot with a beautiful view," he said awkwardly. He was uncomfortable and fumbled for words. This meeting was unusual. Technically, he could face some repercussions for allowing it.

*Yet, she deserved something, didn't she?* He thought to himself.

"I know you expect I am here to chew you out or throw a fit or such. But I'm not," she said and looked at him with a genuine smile. "I wouldn't do that here. And there's not much good that would do."

"The case is still open. The investigation has grown cold, but you never know. Sometimes it just takes one thing to break..." His words faded off as she shook her head slowly, a tear trailing down.

"I already know that. I became a true crime junkie after all that happened. Hell, I became a lot after your visit that night to let me know, the identification was positive."

He still had no words, had no way to relate to the profound loss she had as a mother. He waited for her to continue.

She returned to studying his headstone. "I lost myself in booze, lost my job, nearly lost my girls. My sponsor finally hit home with me. Said that someone stole my child and took the wonderful years he had ahead of him. A life that was meant for great things. I could let this monster keep that or I could take it back. Live my life in honor of my son. Find a positive way to move forward. Not 'move on' but 'move forward'. I liked that!

"I work again, but now from home. I do tax work for six months then the other six I spend with my two girls. I also volunteer at a non-profit organization. We focus on other grieving parents like me. We are a resource to offer therapy, provide networking and even assist in funding for investigations. My life before Mattie was taken was so different... so selfish. I could've been there at the park that day. I thought it was more important for me to finalize a product presentation—"

"No, don't do that, ma'am. I mean, Melissa. Don't put that guilt on yourself. Mattie was targeted. Your good intentions of providing for your family didn't make your son vulnerable to what happened."

"I realize that. It took a lot of soul-searching to find a way to forgive myself for what I had no control over. Anyway, I was a mess, but things have come together after all this time."

She spotted the folders in his hand. "Will those get you in serious trouble, Dax?"

He shrugged. "Nothing I can't handle. In a few years, I am due for a promotion or retirement. Either way, it's not more important than the promise I made to you ten years ago."

Dax handed the copies of the case files over to her. They had his preliminary findings and the police reports of the day her son was taken. Everything he had done then and every step he took after the Feds stepped in.

"What isn't in there is something I cannot give to you in documentation. After his remains were found, the CSI labs found trace amounts of red paint chips on his clothing. The FBI immediately took the case from me going forward."

"Oh, I know. That FBI Taskforce is a black hole. They suck all the information in, any progress, any evidence, everything. Suck it all in and refuse to share any insight with us. Nine years of stonewall silence."

"I have kept tabs with a contact in the Bureau. I can tell you there are no suspects, but there are plenty of rumors and opinions. Seems your son matched with a string of other murders. The red chips of paint, the gender and the age. Even the Tenth month of the year. It all matched –"

"Was he... messed with? Raped?" she asked, her lips quivering.

"They don't think he was. He and the others showed no signs of it."

"Oh, thank God!"

"The taskforce will not release anything to anyone. Should this guy make a mistake, they need the details to be sure they have the right person, you understand. They can't find him yet and they cannot be sure of how many other boys. I am only telling you this as I want you to know I haven't forgotten. Your son still matters to me and a lot of people."

"I didn't doubt your words and your dedication. Yet, after all this time, I really don't need justice. It won't change what happened. My boy was returned to me. I have met parents who have never had their answers, never had closure. I buried my little angel. Do I want the man caught? Of course! But I refuse to let this end my life. I have my girls, and I owe it to them to be there for them too."

She went quiet but continued to quietly weep. That was when he spotted an odd engraving cut into the left corner of the gravestone.

Dax stooped and then squatted down to get a better look at it. It was a QR Code.

"That links to a website I have as memoriam for Mattie. The site has a video we took of him on his last night. He's in his little Frankenstein costume pretending to be scared of the candles on his birthday cake. 'Ooo fire! Fire bad, mommy.' He was so funny and so curious about everything." She went silent again.

"You see, Detective, while that bastard took and killed my son, his spirit remains here in my chest. Living on in my heart where no one can dare ever take him again. Mattie is forever."

Dax rubbed his fingers over the engraving and nodded in agreement.

# BROTHERS BY T.D. BARTON

## Part 1

"Just don't get lost, Kid, okay?" My older brother always called me Kid, or Neighbor Kid. I gained the moniker when I happened to be with him one day while he was hanging out with some of his buddies at Azar's Big Boy, the local drive-in restaurant. They all had motorcycles and were in high school and I wanted so much to be like them. Unfortunately, whenever I spoke up, I always seemed to say the wrong thing and had to endure the embarrassment of their rolling eyes and jeers of derision.

One day one of his friends asked, "Hey, Chuck is this your little brother?" He looked at me as though I were a specimen under a microscope.

"Nah," Chuck answered dismissively. "That's the neighbor kid. Follows me around sometimes." This got big laughs and from then on, I was called Neighbor Kid. I didn't mind though; it was kind of cool that I had been given a nickname. It sort of made me feel like one of the group.

"Stick by my side and try not to be scared," Chuck said as we paid our quarters and got our tickets to the carnival sideshow. The carnivals, during the early sixties were always sure to have a sideshow that exhibited what they called freaks. Chuck and I were excited to see what lay behind the huge canvas walls adorned with paintings so garish and ridiculous as to be almost ludicrous.

One showed the obligatory bearded lady who had to weigh at least seven hundred pounds if one could believe the depiction. She was shown sitting on a tiny stool that impossibly held her weight. Hands on her knees, she wore a simple smock that was cut low in the front to lewdly expose as much cleavage as society would allow. The idea was to show enough to subliminally attract the rubes without getting the carnival shut down and run out of town. Another panel showed an enormous depiction, poorly drawn, of a man with lobster claw hands and feet. He was sitting in the sand on a fictional beach somewhere with a bib around his neck, a bucket, and a toy shovel. Then there was the "geek" that had been captured in the wilds of Borneo whose diet consisted exclusively of reptiles. The poster showed a savage-looking fellow with wild hair and a scraggly beard. He had the rear legs of a frog dangling from his mouth while he was blithely swallowing the front half of the animal. At the same time, he was wrestling with an enormous snake that hung down from the branches of a tree.

There were several of these billboard-sized paintings. Each was more astonishing than the next. All were calculated to attract curious minds, to coerce them to pay the small price and take a look at things that were sure to astonish.

Outside the tent with its fantastic curiosities stood a man with a microphone in his hand screaming to attract customers. "Come on! Come on! Come on!" he barked into the overly loud sound system. "Come see the bizarre! See the fantastic! You'll never forget the unbelievable! You won't believe your eyes!!!" And so on.

Chuck, who at sixteen was six years my senior, held both of our tickets. As we approached the opening of the enormous tent, he handed them off to a scruffy-looking carney who looked as though this was the last place on earth that he wanted to be. The man didn't bother to rip the tickets in two and give us the stubs, he simply dropped the tickets into a bucket that stood in the trampled grass at his feet.

It was dark as we entered the tent, and I resisted the urge to reach up and take my brother's hand. After all, I was ten years old and not a baby anymore. Chuck sensed my unease, however, and leaned over to whisper "Don't worry. This stuff is all fake. You'll see."

The exhibits inside did not disappoint, and we visited each display with rapt attention and wonder. Some of them were obviously fake, but others had us shivering with revulsion or astonished by their bizarre oddities.

The geek from Borneo was indeed there. He sat on the floor of an iron cage wearing nothing but a loin cloth. Repeatedly, he would stuff frogs into his mouth and appear to swallow them. Then he would regurgitate them and smile a disgusting gap-toothed smile. Sometimes he would snarl and rush the bars of the cage, causing everyone to gasp and step back a pace.

As Chuck and I stood there, I overheard another slightly older teenager in the group tell his friend, "Aw, he ain't nothin' but a phony. I saw him driving down Market Street just the other day in a brand-new Cadillac." I thought this was quite funny and I gave a laugh which caused the geek to dash himself against the bars again right in front of me.

The bearded lady turned out to be disappointingly normal once you got over the facial hair. She wasn't nearly as heavy as the poster had shown. Sitting in a regular chair, she answered questions from the audience about what it was like growing up with this affliction. I felt sorry for her but soon became bored.

Moving away from this attraction, I walked over to look down at a display case that purported to house a real-life mummified mermaid. To me, it looked like someone had sewn together the back half of a fish with the top half of a monkey. (It turned out that was exactly what it was.)

When I walked back, the bearded lady was still talking, but Chuck wasn't there. Frantically, I looked around and didn't see him anywhere.

"Chuck!" I called "Hey Chuck!" But I received no answer.

For what seemed like hours to me, but in reality, was probably only twenty or so minutes, I searched the dark crowded tent for my big brother. One bizarre monstrosity after another loomed there in the dark. There was the dog-faced man, the man with elastic skin, and the man they called immortal. He could pierce his body with razor-sharp rapiers and appear to feel not a thing. One after another I stumbled upon frightening inhuman terrors that had me reeling with fear. I managed not to cry, but I was on the verge of tears by the time I found my way to the exit and rushed gratefully out into the sunshine beside the carnival midway.

My eyes were just beginning to adjust when someone grabbed me by the shoulder. With relief, I saw that it was Chuck, who scolded, "What did I tell you? I said to stick with me, didn't I?"

He shook his head in disgust. "C'mon, let's get out of here."


"So that's why I've been afraid of carnival freak shows ever since," I told my friend and co-worker Larry as we sat at the bar of Roscoe's Grill twenty years later. I rattled the ice in my bourbon glass and took another sip. "Now Peebles has me doing a story on that very thing."

Jason Peebles was editor-in-chief of the paper I worked for as an investigative journalist. (Although the title was a bit overblown for the work I did.) The paper was a small one with miniscule circulation and I had the sneaky sensation we wouldn't be in business much longer. The Heath Shows carnival was in town and Peebles thought it would be a good human interest piece. He wanted me to dig into the back stories of some of the carnival's sideshow attractions.

Larry Jackson was the paper's chief photographer. He headed up a small staff of one — meaning he was the only photographer. He was drinking a

Foster's beer and there was an empty sitting off to the side that he was responsible for.

"Sorry I can't come along on this one," he said. "But I'm not about to give up my vacation time for anything."

"No worries," I replied, and I waved my hand. "I can handle it. I *will* need to borrow a camera in case there are any pics to be taken..."

"There's a Minolta in my bottom right-hand desk drawer and plenty of film. Have at it," he said. "Point and shoot." He mimed shooting a picture and made a clicking sound with his mouth.

I tossed down the last of my drink, threw money on the bar, and stood up. "All right then," I smiled. "See ya when you get back."

Part 2

The next day I found myself walking down the midway letting the sights of the carnival take me back to my youth. There was a chaotic combination of sounds: whirring machines propelling the various rides, squeals of those being hurled around and around ad nauseum, and the cries of the carneys to "Take a shot" or "Try three pitches for a dollar" and to "Step right up". All these things together brought a smile to my face. I breathed in the smell of cotton candy and caramel apples. There were fried elephant ears, and corn dogs on a stick. It was a miasma of scents and sounds that blended to nearly overwhelm the senses.

The mixture of children's laughter and musical tones filled the air, and I was surprised to find myself quite happy to be there. I began to regret all the years I had spent avoiding the carnival simply because of that one bad experience.

Then I came to the place I dreaded. Here it was, the huge tent, just adjacent to the midway. Its enormous canvas panels flapped ominously in the breeze and, along with the ever-present carnival barker beckoned me to *Come on! Come on! Come on! Come see the bizarre! See the fantastic! You won't believe your eyes!!!!*

The garish paintings on the canvas panels featured different attractions here in nineteen eighty-five than they had twenty years before, but incredibly they appeared to have been done by the same inept artist.

Now they depicted such exhibits as "The Horse Boy", a person whose knees bent backward, forcing him to walk on all fours. The poster billed him as being half man / half horse. Also shown were the incredible "Bird Lady" a woman said to be covered completely in feathers, and "The Monkey Girl".

At the far end of the panels was pictured the main attraction, the Wassel twins, Bert and Bart, who were joined at the abdomen. Each brother was completely formed but conjoined. They were alike in every way except one: Bert had been born mute.

As I stared at the two baldheaded men depicted on the panel, I became sure that this was the exhibit I needed to interview. I paid my fare (more than twice what it had been before) and went in. I knew it was impossible, but I could swear the same old grizzled carney as the last time took my ticket and dropped it in the bucket.

As before, the entrance was dark and foreboding, intended to put the customer in the right frame of mind. It was effective. Despite myself, I felt the old fears rising and it was all I could do to force my feet to move forward. Slowly, I rounded the corner to find the Bird Lady. It was obvious that she was wearing a costume that featured thousands of feathers glued to it and an intricate makeup job on her hands and face resembling more feathers.

It was laughable and went a great way toward relieving my fear. With a smile on my face, I moved on. I was shocked to discover the same display of the mummified mermaid still being shown although it seemed a bit worse for the wear after all this time.

Shaking my head in wonder I went further and was gratified to see that the next exhibit was the Wassel brothers. They perched side by side on an upholstered bench in a low light situation upon a wooden stage. Thick velvet curtains hung down closely behind and on either side. Two small pedestal-type tables were set at either end supporting identical pitchers of water and a glass tumblers.

There was a group of onlookers gathered about, but I bided my time until they had moved on, and I approached the stage. Bart was having a sip of water from his glass while Bert sat still and silent.

"I beg your pardon," I said, and I cleared my throat as my words had come out somewhat unsteadily. Bart paused in raising his glass and gazed at me mildly.

"Yes?"

I thought that I vaguely got a whiff of some foul odor, but it passed.

"I work as a journalist with the Gazette," I said. "And I was wondering if you would grant me a few moments to interview with you before the next group comes through."

Bart slowly lowered his glass to the table. He seemed to study me for a moment and then said, "Yours was the last group for the day. You may talk with me. However as for Bert..." He nodded knowingly at his twin. "I'm afraid you won't get much out of him."

"Oh, yes, of course," I sputtered, remembering that the poster outside had stated he was a mute. Feeling foolish, I said, "I'm sorry."

"What would you like to know?" Bart asked. His voice sounded highly educated, sophisticated, smooth, and silky, not at all what I had expected. His movements were slow and economical, and Bert didn't seem to move at all.

I held a tablet in my hand and poised a pencil above it.

"Well, where were you born? That is, where are you from?"

"Bert and I were born in the Tyrolian Alps... at the same time."

I had the feeling he was playing with me for his own amusement.

"Right," I said. "Uh, and when was that?"

"My brother and I are thirty-seven years old, although you wouldn't guess it to look at us. I am aware that we appear... older."

I agreed although I didn't say as much.

"So, obviously you were born with your... uniqueness. Have you always belonged to the carnival and if not, what was your life like before you entered, uh, show business?"

The twin smiled, chuckled with a superior air, and said, "Let me save you some time. As children, Bert and I had to learn to do everything together. Walking, talking, eating, sleeping, attending school, everything. You might say we were --- inseparable."

Here he gave out with a throaty chuckle that made me shudder.

"We were the closest of brothers. Nothing could come between us." (Another arrogant smile.) He was pleased with himself.

I remained silent and allowed him to continue.

Our parents were quite wealthy, and we were given everything we might require. We attended the finest schools. Although we had to contend with the inevitable taunts and bullying that one would expect from our classmates, we led a relatively bearable life."

"Then at the age of fifteen our lives took a drastic turn for the worse. Both of our parents were killed in a dreadful accident, and we found ourselves orphaned. You might ask, were there no relatives willing to take us in? But the answer is no. No one was willing to take on two boys with our peculiar differences."

"So, from a life of relative luxury and, you might call it pampering, we were cast out into the streets to fend for ourselves."

He lifted his glass for another sip and returned it to the table. And again, I caught the scent of a foul smell. My nose wrinkled.

"My brother and I wandered the streets of the nearby villages, begging for food and offering to work but as you might expect help was not made readily available. We starved and we suffered as much if not more than any two men ever have, together or singly. Many times, we were beaten or driven away with sticks.

"This horrid life went on for about three years until one day a man named Helfrey came to the village where we were working cleaning out the back room of an inn. Helfrey had heard about us and came to offer us a place in the sideshow of his circus. From there we traveled all over Europe and eventually to America. From one show to another, we worked in the field of entertainment. We saw parts of this world that few men have seen.

"People say that it is degrading to be put on display, like some kind of animal in a zoo. What they don't understand is that this life allows those who work in this industry a chance to make a living. We have a profession and can fully support ourselves and our families. Yes, many of those you see around here who you consider freaks of nature have families. They have feelings and hearts... dreams and desires and all they want is a chance to live their lives. They don't ask to be what you would call normal. They simply want the chance to be human. To be considered as people. Those you call freaks are my family and I will do anything to protect them. They may be different but still, they are people. Do you understand this?"

I nodded.

"While continuing our education on our own, we worked and saved and invested our earnings, eventually amassing a fortune — enough money to buy our own show. That's what this carnival is. The name 'Heath Shows' is just a name to put on the bills. In truth, this is the Wassel Brothers carnival, and we own the whole damn thing.

"There's your story," he said. "That's all you need to know."

I cleared my throat again and put away my notepad. "Thank you both for your time," I said softly.

"Before you leave there is one more thing you should know," Bart said. "My brother Bert was not born a mute. Did you notice that the announcement on the ads outside saying that he was a mute was written with fresher paint than the rest of the sign? We had to add that just so that no one would ask. You see that odor you've been sensing comes from Bert. He's been dead for some time now."

It was at this moment that something hard struck the back of my head, and everything swam out of sight and went black.

Horrible nightmares and grotesque images swarmed in my mind while I was unconscious. I have no idea how long I was out but, eventually, I came to. The first thing I became aware of after regaining consciousness beyond the lightning bolt of agony wracking my head was a searing pain in my mouth. Slowly the terrifying fact came to me that my tongue was missing.

"Yes, my brother," came the silky voice of Bart Wassel. "It's been surgically removed. But don't worry, you won't miss it. I will be there to speak for you whenever you need me."

Stupefied, I ran my hand over my head and discovered that it had been shaved. I blinked my eyes several times and eventually discovered Bart's face swimming into view incredibly near. He was staring at me with an insanely loving expression.

"Hello, Brother," he said. "Glad you could join me. One of the benefits of amassing a large fortune is that I've been able to employ some of the most advanced, creative surgeons in the world to help me when I need them. And this time I needed them very badly indeed.

"With Bert passing away, I found my own life expectancy to be extremely shortened. His deterioration was in the process of poisoning my blood. Normally I would have been dead within hours from sepsis. However, my doctors found a way to isolate the poison and prevent it from entering my system. Still, this would only be temporary. I had to find a replacement, or I was soon to pass on myself. We couldn't let that happen now, could we?" Again, he chortled that disgustingly sinister laugh, the one that made my skin crawl.

"So, you see, my doctors have kept me alive against all odds and performed a veritable miracle by removing the dead tissue and by giving me a new brother."

Horrified, I opened my mouth in a silent scream. Nothing came out except a gurgle.

"Now, now, hush my brother," Bart soothed. "I realize this may have been a bit of a shock for you but in time you will accept it and come to appreciate life in the entertainment field. It's really quite amusing. And just you wait and see ... we're going to be *very* close."

# TIP LINE                                BY BRIAN GATTI

## Part 1

The phone on my desk vibrated, rang, and flickered, displaying an unusual number - 048621 RNTN.

I slowed my breathing, grabbed a notepad with a blank page, and pressed the Accept Call button.

With a calmness I've never truly felt, I said, "My name is Jenny. You've been kidnapped, and I don't know who did it. I didn't do this to you and don't know why I am involved. I will do my best to help you survive this labyrinth. It is crucial for you to describe everything to me and answer my questions completely. I cannot guarantee I can help you make it, but the information you share may save the next person's life."

The connection crackled, and I held my breath, waiting for the voice, bracing myself. Would they cry? Scream? Beg? Blame me?

There was a sniffle on the other end of the line. "Hello?" A woman's voice, young sounding. A faint southern twang, maybe Georgia?

"Hi. What's your name?"

"I'm Anna. Anna Baysen. What's going on? Where am I?"

I was surprised at how calm she sounded. "Anna, I need you to focus. You don't have a lot of battery life on your phone, and you need to take notes. Can you do that?"

There was some rustling noise and another sniffle. "Uh-huh. Write what?"

"Your life is in danger. You're in a maze, and it's designed to kill you. Do you understand? This is deadly serious. I will try to help you, but we have to work together. Ok?" I kept all emotion from my voice. She seemed to have accepted her situation for now. I wanted her to remain determined.

"Are you the police?"

"No, I'm not. But we are going to do our best to get you out. Now start writing."

I started by giving her detailed instructions to get her to the end of the first section of the labyrinth. "Everything I outlined you can do by feel, OK? So turn the phone off to save battery. Don't use it as a flashlight if you can avoid it, OK?"

"Yes... I understand. Thank you, Jenny." Then, the call ended.

It's been the same thing for months now. I've had to listen to forty-six people die. So many lives have been lost, and I have no idea why.

It always starts with a strange call from a number attached to a burner phone. One man, Jamal, victim #27, said it looked like a knock-off Nokia. The victim wakes up in a dark room with a notebook, a pen, and a phone. The phone's sole saved contact says Tip Line, which dials my number. The phone is always charged to 23% and can only ever call my number.

They never know why they are there, and they have no memory. They're from all over the US, and a few were tourists, but were all trapped in that murderous labyrinth.

My first call was from Theresa, a schoolteacher and mother of three from Hartford, Connecticut. She hadn't survived more than three minutes when she stumbled across a claymore mine planted in one dead end. One second, we were talking; the next, there was a sharp sound and nothing.

I've heard the prayers, curses, tears, and final moments. The weight of my failures used to crush me to the point where I couldn't breathe. The only thing that kept me going was the idea that I was their only hope.

Poor bastards.

Part 2

Who am I? I'm Jennifer Pierce of the Chicago Pierces. A storied family renowned for producing successful entrepreneurs and attorneys like China produces plastic crap to sell to the world.

Except for little old Jenny, the oldest and most disappointing child. The unworthy heir to a great line of powerful men and women.

I'd been living on my own, failing as a graphic designer and dodging the constant attempts of my grandmother, the matriarch of our clan, to fix my life. To give me focus and purpose.

Well, I have those things now.

The phone lights up with 048621 RNTN.

"Anna, what's the battery at?" This is always my first question. Battery life equals their life.

"19%," she replied softly. "I think I'm in the right place. There's a box here with half a bottle of water and a granola bar."

I exhaled with relief. Nineteen was a healthy number. We had a chance. "Good job. You're doing it. Just to make sure, did you have to make two lefts to get into the room you're in?"

"Yes," she replied, a shiver in her voice. "I'm thirsty. I'm going to drink some of this water."

"It's safe, as long as you made two lefts to get there."

Another victim, Morgan, victim #7, taught me there was a false cache down a similar path. I heard him gurgle and scream as he drank what I presumed was acid. Did you know there are potent acids that will burn through glass but not specific types of plastic? I didn't, but I do now.

There was scraping as she moved and audible drinking sounds. I waited about thirty seconds and said, "Anna, I need you to take notes now. Battery life is your life. You'll need to use the phone as a flashlight for the next part, ok?"

Something hollow and plastic thumped on the ground. A whispered, "Shit," and then louder, she said, "Ok, I'm ready."

I outlined the next fifteen minutes of her life, including a trapped puzzle as one of her obstacles. "Jenny, am I gonna see my mom again?"

These questions made my chest ache. "We are gonna do our best, Anna. You leave, and we will meet up and get drinks. Ok?" I kept the preemptive grief out of my voice, but my throat hurt from the effort.

"I want a Long Island iced tea, maybe three."

I laugh a little to encourage her moments for levity and then return to business. "Anna, I know it feels lonely, but I must hang up now. You need your battery for the puzzle. Ok?"

A sniffled acknowledgment came, and then the call disappeared from my display. I exhaled sharply and waited.

When everything first started, I called my parents in a pure panic. You'd think someone kidnapped the president's daughter. My father deployed the sizable resources of the Pierce clan to investigate. Grandmother refused to involve the FBI and said they'd assume I was an accessory. In retrospect, this sounds stupid, but it's definitely true now.

The best trackers and hackers were deployed to find the source. The calls stopped. After three weeks of intensive search and no results, they stopped looking. The second call came the next day.

I sank into depression so deep I tried to end my life. It was the third call, a woman named Andrea. She just lay in the first room and cried. I listened as she begged for her life, to see her baby boy again. She whimpered as the phone battery died. I have no idea what became of her. Did she die from thirst? Did a trap take her?

I drowned in her despair, unable to breathe. I took a bottle of pills. I only survived because my mom came by to check on me. I was in the hospital and then in intensive therapy. Mercifully, there were no calls then.

I checked the clock. She should be halfway through. I can't shake the cold, oily dread that settles in my gut whenever I have to wait.

I realized after my recovery from my suicide attempt that I was also trapped, and I'd only escape when the prisoners did. After that moment, I made this my focus. When the calls started again, I drew maps of the labyrinth and took detailed notes on what the people experienced. I also wrote their names on my wall, like a memorial to their senseless deaths. Someone should remember them so their families could one day know what became of them.

Earlier than expected, the phone lit up.

"Anna, I'm here."

There was a sob on the other end. "Oh god, Jenny, my fucking leg. It got my fucking leg! I can't stop the bleeding. Help me, please! God help me."

I closed my eyes. She must've gotten caught in the trap somehow. "Can you rip your pant leg off and make a tourniquet? I can walk you through it. You just need to breathe and be calm."

The connection crackled. A voice like a frightened child came through, "I can't. My hand is broken, I think. I can't move my right hand." A shivering sob. "I'm tired, and it hurts Jenny. I'm sorry. I can't do it. I need to lay down. Just let me rest for a moment."

Pain erupted up my throat in a tearing sob. "Please, Anna. Try. Please. We have a chance. Please."

"You're kind. Thank you for helping me. I hope you make it." Her voice sounded far away, vacant. "Tell my husband that -"

Call ended.

Her phone died, leaving Anna alone in the dark to die.

I shrieked in rage and frustration. The bubbles of hysteria swirled inside me, and I clenched my jaw like I was trying to hold back vomit. "You love him. Tell your husband you love him. When this is over, I will!"

Part 3

It took me three days to recover from Anna. Well, recovery is a lie. When you have to listen to the deaths of forty-eight strangers, it leaves you with scars that'll never heal. I can't even imagine how fucked up I am.

My family doesn't know it's still going on. I lied after I got out of the hospital. They're paying for everything right now because they think I'm getting over the trauma of my suicide attempt.

You know, the people in the labyrinth are what keep me going. I want to catch the miserable piece of trash that's responsible for it all.

I have this idea that the answer is at the end — the key to making it stop.

As I went through my morning routine, my phone vibrated. I glanced down at the display and saw a text.

051621 RNTN - This is your last chance. If you fail, you will be the next one fed to the labyrinth.

Numbness spread through me at the cold white words on the black display.

There was an incoming call - 0520621 RNTN.

I took a breath and raised the phone to my ear, "My name is Jenny. You've been kidnapped, and I don't know who did it. I didn't do this to you and don't know why I am involved. I will do my best to help you survive this labyrinth. It is crucial for you to describe everything to me and answer my questions completely. I cannot guarantee I can help you make it, but the information you share may save the next person's life."

A heartbeat and then a woman's voice. "Jenny?" Another breath, labored and afraid, "Honey, is that you?"

The world stopped and coldness filled me. "Mom?" I almost choked on the word.

Silence.

"Mom?" I asked again, panic rising.

"Oh shit, Jenny..." She whispered. It was weird but it struck me that I'd never heard her swear before. "Where am I? What's happening? What are you doing?"

The coldness grew, metamorphosing from terror to resolve as I realized the timer was running. There was no time for doubt and indecision. No time for her to panic and question and wonder. There was only time to focus and obey.

"Stop Claudia, right now." I intentionally used her name to disassociate a little and to break her mental maelstrom of panic. "To your left, against the wall, is a notebook and a pencil. Get it, now."

Some faint scratching as she moved, her rapid breathing audible in the small room. I could see it so clearly in my mind's eye, as though I were there. Her manicured hand groped in the dark, looking for the battered notebook and pencil. Finally, "I've got them."

"You're in danger. You have to do everything I say the way I say it. No questions, no debate. Write this down as quickly as you can."

"I'm ready," she said, her voice quavering.

I rattled off the first fifteen minutes of instructions. A precise step-by-step, an outline to escape written in the blood of the forty-eight victims that came before. Despite all the madness, I felt more in control than I ever had, so assured.

Once she confirmed she'd written everything down, I said, "OK, turn the phone off when I hang up. You're going to need to navigate in the dark to save as much battery as possible. When you get to the last part in my directions, turn the phone back on and call me. Understand?"

"Yes," she sobbed softly. "I love you, sweetheart!" Then the call disconnected.

I immediately called my father and got his voicemail. I called his secretary. Father was in a meeting with a client, but she would interrupt since it was an emergency. I called grandmother next.

"Grandmother, it's Jenny! Someone has kidnapped my mother," I began without preamble.

"What are you saying?" Her voice was reedy with age but held none of the weakness of the elderly. "Slow down Jenny and explain."

I gave her a quick run-through of the situation I'd been in and what I thought was happening with Mom. I could hear her listening attentively, not interrupting me.

At the end, she sounded surprisingly calm. "I understand. It sounds as though time is of the essence. I will call our private security firm immediately and have them get on it. You continue helping her, as it sounds like you're able. We may not have enough time for the firm to take action, but we'll try."

I was unsurprised by this response. What could they do? They didn't even know where she was. I certainly had no clue. "Thank you, Grandmother."

Then I dropped off and went to the wall, studying the maps again and guessing where Mom was in the progress. It hurt, not knowing. Would I hear from her? Would she make a mistake? The cold resolve I felt before was replaced with sick worry as I envisioned the pampered woman being forced to crawl through the torture maze.

Thirteen minutes passed when the phone rang. It was Mom's phone, not my dad's.

"Mom? Are you ok?"

A shuddering breath greeted me. "I got hit by something. I think shotgun pellets. It hurts, but I was far enough away for most to miss me." There was a rustle as I heard her shift the phone. "I have the notebook ready. The phone is down to 6% already."

Shit! It should only be down to 8% at this point.

"Did you turn it on at some point before calling me?" I asked, concerned.

"Yes, I'm sorry. I couldn't see... I was scared." She sounded like a little girl, her voice pleading for forgiveness.

"You cannot let your weakness and lack of focus control you," I said, my words sharp. "You're going to *fucking die*, Claudia, unless you follow my instructions precisely. Do you understand?"

A sucking sob was all I got back.

"Write this down. You have 30 minutes of instructions here. The trick is to be slow and deliberate..." I outlined the pattern of the pressure plates down the hall she was facing and to ignore the sounds of running water. It was a red herring, and a trap combined. I warned her about the trip wire at the end of the third tunnel.

"Do not use the phone again until you reach the end of the third tunnel. Then call me."

I hung up the phone and waited. The time crawled with agonizing slowness. I called my father's office again. The secretary informed me that Grandmother had called and briefed Father He was headed to her house. The security team was working furiously. The FBI had also been contacted. Stephen, the cybersecurity guy, was also working through his NSA contacts.

Thirty minutes passed. Then thirty-five. Nothing.

Finally, after thirty-eight minutes had ticked away, the phone rang.

"What percentage are you at?"

"4." She replied.

"OK." I swallowed. We were approaching the end of my notes and map. The last four never made it past the next leg, what I hoped would be the last part of the labyrinth.

"The tunnel branches left and right. I think the correct direction is right, though no one has survived past this point. I know the tunnel has some kind of gas in it that causes dizziness and vomiting. There may be a gap or something on the side because I heard someone stumble and fall."

"Alright. I'm listening," she said, her voice broken and tired.

"Go right. Take a deep breath and hold it. You need as much oxygen as possible. I don't know how long the tunnel is. Stay in the middle. Walk carefully. Slow is fast here. Your lungs may start hurting, but you can't breathe until you make it past the tunnel. Then call me, I'm not sure what comes next, but we'll figure it out together."

"I love you, Jenny."

I drew breath to reply but the call disconnected. I cried.

Three minutes passed like torture. A text from grandmother. They may have a lead. More to come.

My phone lit up and it said 0520621 RNTN.

"Mom??"

"I made it through Jenny," she whispered. "The battery is at 1%. There is a door, but it's locked. Nowhere else to go. Only numbers."

"What numbers? Read them to me!"

Some movement and then she said, "41 degrees 40 apostrophe, 58.4 inches then the letter N."

I stared stupidly at what I had written down. Then it hit. GPS coordinates. "Hurry. Is there a second set of numbers? Fast! It must be your location."

"I have it. 88 degrees 16 minutes, 4--" Then the call died.

I shrieked in frustration. FUCK!

I pulled up the numbers on Google Earth, guessing at the directions. Two put the spot in Lake Michigan (unlikely), one was in the middle of Chicago and the other was a small open field outside the city.

[190]

I texted the Chicago address to my grandmother and said I would head to the other. I called my family's car service and ran downstairs to meet the driver.

The location was an hour outside of town, the longest ride of my life. My grandmother kept in touch with me, advising they were in communication with the building owners. She stated that a private security team would meet me at the other location.

We finally pulled up near the location. Missing the final decimal of the GPS would mean searching.

The private security team was about fifteen minutes behind us, but I couldn't wait. The idea of my mother trembling in the dark labyrinth of the Minotaur was too much to bear any longer.

I pushed out of the car and moved through the sea of tall grass toward a low-slung building made of metal sheets. The door hung on its last hinge as I tore it open. Its rusted metal shrieked.

I turned on my flashlight and saw the floor was dirt, unfinished space. Semi-organized piles of junk were everywhere. Blindly, I moved past it, eyes searching for a door.

Hidden partially behind a set of blue barrels were concrete stairs that descended below the dirt floor, a metal door at the bottom.

Everything became blurry for me as I headed down the stairs. There was a simple twist deadbolt at the bottom. I snapped it in the open position and pulled the door.

Something fell against my leg.

I looked down and saw my mother, prone on the ground, fallen over. I thought she was dead, but her body moved with shaky breaths. "Mom! It's Jenny. Please, wake up."

I knelt and lifted her head, her confused eyes looking at me. "Baby?" She murmured and touched my face, as though I were a hallucination. "Oh, baby!" Mom reached up, clutched at my shirt, and pulled herself toward me, sobbing in relief and terror.

"You're safe, but we need to get you out of here! The private security team should be here soon."

Then I heard the sound of clapping behind me. My head jerked around and standing there at the top of the steps was the slender form of my grandmother. The expression on her face was hard to read. Behind her stood my father, his head bowed as usual.

"Well done, Jenny." Grandmother said to me, her thin lips twisted into the approximation of a smile. "Well done."

"Wh-what?" I stammered in shock, standing up with my mother. "What the fuck is happening?" I felt outrage building inside.

"You did it. Completed your course. I admit, I was certain you wouldn't have it in you, but you made it. The Pierces always rise to the occasion." Her head was held haughtily, her pale blue eyes looked into mine. "I am so impressed. Listening to your calls with your mother, the firmness. The direction. The focus and leadership."

Grandmother looked at Father, "What do you think, Winston? Did your daughter pass?"

Father nodded and stepped to stand beside my grandmother, mimicking her expression and proud stance. "My girl? Yes! She has passed. Of course, only servants are told what to do. Now she must accept it all for us to be finished."

Grandmother nodded and looked back at me.

Perplexed, I shook my head in horror.

"All those people... did they die or was it all just a test — a ruse?" I stuttered. "Did you allow me to think I had killed all those victims as some sort of... family indoctrination?"

"We had to be sure you measured up to the level of a Pierce," Grandmother explained, her voice overly patient and condescending. She descended the stairs to reach out and lay her cold, palsied hand against my fevered cheek.

"We have great plans for you. As our future leader of the Pierce clan, you will wield great authority. You will head up giant corporations and collude with politicians and leaders of countries — men and women of great power. You will be the one to see that the name of Pierce continues to help control the world. But we had to test your mettle first, dear. Don't you see?"

I turned to look at my mother and found her standing, smiling tenderly at me. She appeared unharmed and was standing.

"Try to understand, Baby. This was for your own good. It made you stronger, showed your gifts," she said. And I realized she had been in on it all along.

"Mom?" I sobbed. "Mother?"

I realized that I didn't know any of these people who stood around me looking so pleased with themselves. All I knew was that they had put me through hell and that I hated them. Despised them. I had nearly killed myself over the remorse I had felt and now knew to be only an ugly trick. I would not accept what they wanted from me. I would not play along with their twisted game. I would rather see them all dead.

"NO!" I shrieked. "I'll NEVER —" With an anguished scream, I launched myself at the shriveled, evil old shrew, but I didn't get far. Father put himself between us. Then two of her towering security officers grabbed me before I could get any closer. I felt a prick in the side of my neck and the world swam away into black.

Part 4

When I awoke, I was in total darkness. The room around me felt close, suffocating. I gently shook my head, trying to clear the cobwebs. A faint stench assaulted my senses. I didn't recognize the source.

As my equilibrium began to return, my heart pounded as I determined where I must be. Reaching out with a trembling hand, I felt around in the pitch black until I discovered a notebook and a pen. Beside these two items was a cell phone which I quickly snatched up. When I opened the screen, I saw to my horror that there was only the predictable 23% charge. Gasping, I checked the contacts to find there was only one. It was my number. It was Grandmother's way of telling me that I would not have any help. I was on my own.

*They won't get away with this! I won't let—*

My anger and thoughts were blasted away when the light from the cell phone lit up a body lying only a few feet from me. I slowly revealed more details with the flashlight. There was a pair of dusty, black Converse sneakers, faded denim jeans, and then a torn orange tee shirt with a Denver Broncos logo. In their left hand, they cradled another cell phone. The skin of the arm was blackened and desiccated down to the bones. The shriveled and decrepit woman had cobwebs tangled in her blonde curly hair and attached to her black-rim glasses...

"Oh God, it's Andrea!" I gasped with realization. The third victim who had given up, wailing that she wanted to see her son again. She had simply died at the start of the labyrinth.

*It was all real! All those deaths! ...NO! All those murders!* My mind screamed in fury and outrage.

"I will not add to your body count! You will not have my death! Grandmother! Father! Mother! I am going to get out of here and expose you for the monsters you are!" My words echoed and rang out into the darkness.

My trembling had stopped. I was no longer afraid. I had a newfound purpose.

I breathed in three deep breaths, calming and focusing my mind. I placed my hand on the handle of the first door. All the tunnels, the traps, the puzzles, their solutions, were all in my memory. I had this!

The handle began to heat up as waves of smoke billowed in at my feet under the door. I could hear the faint crackle of wood burning somewhere within the tunnels.

They had torched it. Everything, everyone.

*Of course! Grandmother, you always said, 'Leave nothing to chance. Always be absolute.'*

*You bitch!*

## IT GROWLS FROM THE CORNER BY DEREK BARTON

I leaned over and slowly turned the faucet, watching the tepid water pouring into the tub. I sat for a moment absorbed in my thoughts. My world had taken a major hit and nosedived. It all happened right here. Somehow, he turned my own home into a nightmare!

Unable to stop myself, I focused on the cuts and bruises on my hands and arms. A nasty laceration on the top of my left wrist was especially worrisome. It was jagged and deep, held together by twenty-some stitches. A jarring flash image of Jeff's knife crossed my mind. It had been serrated. One of those hunting knives he collected.

I gasped despite myself as an ugly thought bubbled up. What if it was the knife that I bought him for Christmas two years ago? Would he have done that? I couldn't recall what the gift had looked like. Before that night, I would have never thought he could be that cruel. Now, I couldn't honestly profess that I knew Jeff Huntington at all.

My hand hesitated as I reached for the shower control lever. First, I glanced at the floor and then stood, pulled off two long white towels from the rack, and laid them out on the gray linoleum. I would never shower behind a curtain again. The bloody and torn-up shower liner from before remained untouched from where it had been wadded up and thrown into the corner by the sink.

Son-of-a-bitch has robbed me of that too. I once cherished long hot showers. Never again. That was exactly how that night had started.

I had driven home after 3 pm from my waitress job at the truck stop, dropped everything, and jumped right into the shower. My uniform always reeked of Anthony's greasy food and the hated smell coated my skin. It was a habit, the first thing I did every night.

Jeff knew that.

I never heard him come into the bathroom. He must have hidden somewhere in the house. When we broke up three weeks ago, I had demanded the key back, but he obviously must have made a copy.

Right after the lights went out in the bathroom, he started swinging his aluminum baseball bat. He caught me square on the right side with his first swing. It broke two ribs. However, he didn't stop with one swing. I was soaking wet, bleeding, screaming, and crying as he carried me out and into the bedroom. There he had already fastened nylon rope to the bed frame. More beating rendered me semi-conscious. I was barely aware when Jeff bound my hands and feet.

Up to that point, Jeff had not said a single word. He shook me to a somewhat lucid state. "You did all this," he said with a sneer. His voice was terse, his jaw clenched. "You brought all of this on, you understand? It isn't up for debate. No arguing. You just don't have the right to call it quits. *I* am the man! Okay? You are the woman! *I* will say when and if you can leave. Got that? And Teresa, you aren't leaving ME!"

He brutally raped me for hours in between breaks to pound his fists into my stomach or cut my body with his blade.

If my two co-workers, Barbara and Shawn, hadn't come by to take me out dancing as usual on Friday nights, he probably would have killed me. The police believed the coward fled unseen out the backdoor. I was completely knocked out at that point and bleeding badly. It was early in the morning when I woke up days later in the hospital ICU bed.

Unable to realistically stall any longer, I forced myself to take my first shower since his assault. Maybe baths will be more to my taste in the future? I gingerly stepped into the hot water and rotated the shower lever. The water did feel good as I had only had sponge baths for most of my hospital stay. But it was still too fresh. An open wound not scabbed over. Even with the curtain missing I felt my heart race. I grew anxious, too frightened to close my eyes. Every door and window was locked and secured. I made sure every light in the house was on and all the drapes pulled tightly closed.

He was still out there hiding somewhere in the city. They hadn't found him yet. Hell, he could still be hiding here waiting to finish his baseball practice and end my life once and for all.

I stopped the shower and grabbed another towel to dry off. Right then I craved – needed – a strong drink. I will never feel safe again.

As I entered the doorway, I caught sight of my reflection in the mirror above the sink. My right eye remained puffed up like a large plum. Three lines of stitches marred my left cheek and the bridge of my nose. My bare skin was exposed in patches where he cut chunks of my red hair from my scalp. Two of my front teeth were missing. Now I knew why they refused to let me go to the hospital floor bathroom. My personal unit's room's mirror had been removed. I hadn't even noticed.

"Ohhh. Ohhhh. God, what did you do to me?" I barely recognized myself.

I spent hours weeping into my pillows before I passed out from exhaustion and the meds the hospital had given me.

\* \* \*

Someone said something. Calling me?

I rolled over onto my back, wincing from sudden sharp pain. The broken ribs were not letting me off that easily and punished me for forgetting them. My breath came out shaky and plumed in the frigid air of the bedroom.

Huh? It's summer!

I shot a look at the window in the southern corner of the bedroom. It was dark outside, and only the streetlights glowed through the beige curtains. The room was pitch black. The hall light was off as well. My hands gripped the sheets in a surge of panic.

Is he back?

A low growl wafted through the room. An ominous patch of pure darkness occupied the corner opposite the window. The patch completely blotted all of the room's features. Something inside it smelled almost like rotting garbage or old meat. It was truly rank, and I couldn't help but gag. Yet, I couldn't compel myself to move. A pair of silvery eyes opened slowly inside the black patch in the corner. They didn't move, only stared intently and deliberately.

Oh god, what do I do now? I can't fight him off... Wait! Is that Jeff? What is that?

My frantic thoughts raced, but my body remained locked and rigid under the sheets.

"Wh-wh-who?" The word slipped out from chapped and split lips.

No reply. No movement. Nothing.

I waited several long and drawn-out minutes.

"I see you," I stated. This time with no stammer, but the fright still had its grip on my heart. "What do you want?"

The patch grew larger. I heard sharp claws scrape against the tiles of the bedroom floor. It made a full exhale of fetid breath before it leaped into the air and landed deftly upon my chest. This shadow beast pinned me to the bed. Razor-sharp points of its claws poking into the pajama top I wore. It was heavy but not unbearable. The patch was now child-size and perched on my trembling body. A dark, blurry face, lean and elongated like a goat with two big watery eyes peered down at me. The creature tilted its head to one side. Wide, black antlers clicked against the wall.

"Are you tired, Teresa?" it asked. The voice was slightly nasal but had a smooth humanlike tone and resonance.

"Wh-what?" I replied, again stammering uncontrollably.

"Tired of always being beaten, put upon. Broken. Your whole life you have lived under someone's thumb. First Daddy. Then Uncle Ron after your parents died. Later, you let one loser after another take piece after piece of Teresa Rianne Baylor. Did Jeff take the last bit of you? Are you dead after all?"

The haunting words dug deep, shredding my spirit and soul. Tears poured down my sliced cheeks.

"Are you there?" It inquired.

"Yes. Yes to all your questions."

"Good. Yes. There you are." It leaned down between furry haunches that I briefly glimpsed in the shadowy patch. The goat face was merely inches from mine. Wisps of black fur on its chin tickled my neck. "Is there enough of you left to finally make a stand? Make them pay. Make them know who they are dealing with?"

I didn't know how to respond.

"You will never be powerless again. You don't have to feel pain like that."

I nodded. Then whispered, "How?"

"Give me shelter."

"You want to stay here?" I was lost in the direction of the conversation.

A low rumbling growl from deep within the beast's chest evolved into a chuckle. "No, no, not this shit hole." A bony, pale gray index finger came down and pointed to my forehead. "Shelter." There was a tangible electricity to the spoken word. I could almost feel the weight of it drop onto my chest from its mouth.

Is this a nightmare? It can't be real!

*Oh, girl, I am very real.* Its voice rang out inside my skull.

"Please! Please don't hurt me," I wailed. This was all too much, too sudden after the terror that Jeff had put me through.

*STOP!* It demanded. Its dead-cold finger with a nail, black as oil and crusted with gore, pressed into my skin.

My words stopped short, my mouth closed, and I gazed in awestruck wonder up at the demonic face.

"Shelter me and you will never walk alone again. Never be weak again. You will face the world fearlessly. SHELTER ME. SERVE ME NOW. I WILL THEN STOP HIM AND THE OTHERS...FOREVER...

A simple smile formed on my busted lips. I felt a part of myself return. A flicker of life was restored.

A dark calm passed through my ravaged body as my master smiled a toothy, frothy grin.

\* \* \*

A loud series of snores vibrated through the trailer, even shaking the walls with their powerful volume. I found the fat pig passed out, slouched onto his left side in a broken recliner. Beer cans were crumpled at his feet, a discarded bag of Doritos lay on the floor and only a muted television set on a crate lit up the room.

Jeff was back home, carefree with all charges dropped. The investigation died since they couldn't find me. Some even suspected Jeff had found me first and I was rotting somewhere in a shallow grave. Or some think it was a ploy by me to get attention or a smear campaign because Jeff is such an upright citizen. Either way, there was no one to testify and no one to accuse him. The police apologized and sent him on his way scot-free. Without a doubt, they were fearing he was going to sue their asses for false arrest.

That was all fine. I didn't want the police to keep Jeff. He was all alone now.

The air thickened as the temperature dropped. Jeff's snores subsided some when he hugged his arms across his wide chest and shivered. All but the light from the television darkened, snuffed out under a blanket of silence. A rotating fan standing next to the doorway cruised to a stop.

Jeff didn't hear the soft whine coming from Cooper, his aged beagle, as he slinked out of the room. His tail was tucked between his legs in resignation and fear.

An infinite patch of darkness swallowed even more light from the room and the shadow expanded above the television set.

Jeff woke up with a start. Tangled fragments of a nightmare drifted away as he blinked himself awake. *I plagued his dreams.*

His eyes focused on an old rerun of the Password game show. The colors from the screen had bled away, now only stark blacks and whites were visible. The people were also distorted, their heads elongated as their arms stretched in odd angles. *My visit was distorting reality, bending the rules.*

"What the Hell?" he murmured, fascinated yet seemingly repulsed by the surreal sight.

I let out a soft hiss that broke his concentration, and he noticed then the patch of utter darkness above the set for the first time. The patch had settled and now appeared crouching on top of his television. *It was time for me to enter.*

I showed my two slender hands and altered them to an abnormal length. His eyes bulged at the sight. Then my thin fingers slowly inched their way down. My new blood-red nails made tiny clicking sounds on the glass of the screen until they reached the crate. My hands were still pale and feminine, but I kept the cuts and bruises he made. They crisscrossed and wrapped about my limbs. That long laceration that twisted around the wrist especially caught his attention.

Jeff reflexively sat up and pulled his legs away from the crate. He trembled now with fear more than from the chill.

My soft laughter at the sight of him drowned out his disbelief. "Oh, God. Teresa?"

"Mmm-hmmm. Baby, I'm home. I'm hurt. It doesn't look like you missed me." My distorted voice was high-pitched and purposefully mocking.

His hands scrambled and plucked a long knife that was sheathed at his belt. He waved it before him. "I will mess you up! Don't get near me!"

I laughed even louder at his silly show of bravado. He was about to see who he was up against. I expanded the patch more and manifested. I was taller and slender than I was before. A lot of me had changed!

I slid down and flowed out toward him like watery smoke as the television blinked dead without a sound. His entire trailer was dark and dense as a tomb.

"You did all this," I said. "You brought all of this on, you understand? It isn't up for debate. No arguing. You just don't have the right to call it quits tonight. I am in control now, little man. You are *my* bitch! *I* will say when and if you live. Got that? And Jeff, you will never be leaving me!"

I erupted in more malicious gales of laughter as my hand slashed out impossibly fast. The strike flayed open his right cheek. The skin and flesh slipped down and folded over exposing teeth and upper jawbone.

It was the first of Jeff's bloodcurdling screams, but not the last he was going to give to me.

The last screams came when I squeezed my fingers into his skull and plucked out his eyes one by one and then laid them perfectly on top of the television facing the door.

I left him alive for now. When the police found him, he was blind, castrated, amputated, and mute. Lying in a pool of his own blood. I did leave him with his hearing intact. I wanted him to hear the whispers of pity, and the placating lies that they would tell him. Their useless efforts to save him as he was rushed to the hospital. The same one that saved my life.

But his soul could not be saved. That was *mine* now...

BONUS STORY CONTENT...

BLIGHT HOTEL                          BY DEREK BARTON

The water left lines of mud upon my face and neck. It tasted metallic and bitter. It was ice cold, leaving my skin red and stinging. I choked and sputtered the water from my lips as I rolled onto my back. Flood water continued to rush over and around me.

*Where was I?* Every muscle felt stiff and sore. Every inch of my body hurt at once. Every breath was a struggle to take in. *What happened to me?*

My eyelids slowly pulled apart. Above me were black and gray violent skies that pounded rain down in hard sheets. A series of lightning flashes lit up the looming building standing only feet away. I was in the gutter of a bleak, empty street.

Nothing made sense nor had memory illuminated anything of the hours before this moment.

My eyes scoured the building façade's gray, dark green, and black bricks. It was constructed of an ordinary brick, nothing complicated about the pattern, but there was something intangible about it. A threatening aura. A malevolent air. An ominous presence. It didn't know who I was, why I dared to be on its property, and it promised misery for me for the slightest cause. Patches of wild fungus and purplish vein-like vines grew in clusters upon it like barnacles on old log piers.

My eyes continued to investigate its shadowy construction. The building stood at least thirty stories high and nearly a block long. The ground floor had only an entry of twin, silver metal doors. They were braced with iron and a broken chain woven around the handles. There was nothing else but a solid wall for that first floor.

The second floor as well as the others had tall, amber glass windows with tiny triangular patios every twenty or so feet. There were black wooden shutters and rusting iron frames about the windows, but it was plain and nondescript. They were too high for me to see inside. I could only make out golden light glowing from inside but little of it escaped through the thick window glass.

The structure was ugly and brutish. If it had been a man, you would move your child behind you, walk across the street, or find a sudden reason to walk in the opposite direction. You would not chance your child near him! You didn't know it's cause or reasons, you just knew it meant harm and violence.

The muddy puddle continued to deepen about my shivering form as the rain grew even harder.

I could stay and die on the ground or move forward. My choice. The menacing structure didn't care. It waited for my action first. Its first impression of me was already decided.

I used my stiff arms to push myself halfway up to a sitting position. My left dress shoe was gone, the green sock wet and caked with slimy, wet earth. The right shoe was torn, and the heel hung partially off to the side.

Blood bubbled out the side of my mouth and ran down my chin. My tongue was cut and one of my incisors was broken at the root. Searing pain thrummed along my jaw. Its intensity was magnified by all the other pain my body was already suffering.

I also saw that I wore the remains of an expensive black tux. The slacks were ripped beyond repair down one seam. The once bleached bone-white shirt was now splattered with blood and literally soiled from lying on the ground.

Next to my leg was a once-expensive gold wristwatch. Its brown leather band was broken and snapped. The crystal face had been shattered and sheared away.

It was obvious that I had dressed for a fine affair. Yet my current condition had not been the expected outcome for the night.

I glanced to the right. There was a wide three-lane street. It was flooding severely with brackish stormwater. On the other side, were twin boarded-up shops. Maybe at one time a record store or book shop combo. I couldn't tell. The signs hanging above their glass doors were too faded to read. A rundown boarded-up movie theater sat decomposing next to the shops. It had no signs of life. Another wooden corpse exposed to the storm.

*What the hell? Where was everyone?* The entire street was empty and abandoned.

Only the tempest above raged and railed against the ugly...hotel? Or was it an apartment complex?

It had no signs on it or the murky land in front of it. Perhaps they were carried off by the flood water.

There were no cars either. No one was driving or even evacuating to higher ground level. No neglected beaters or rust buckets parked on the side.

I found my feet. Stood trembling. Doubt and confusion blurred any coherent thought. I didn't know where I was, what happened to me, or even my name!

On wobbly legs, I shambled to the doors ahead of me. Flood water had reached mid-shin. The chain on the door handles rattled and fell noisily into the water. With caution, I gripped the handle, and it gave way easily enough as if it offered refuge at the same time daring me to come inside.

Water poured in but the lobby floor already had several inches. I could hear streams of ceiling leaks echoing in the pitch dark. A ghastly sour stench wafted out toward me. The air inside was chilled, rancid, and left your skin feeling greasy.

The ugly complex had not had recent visitors despite the lamp light I saw on the other floors.

I had to find the last of my strength to shove the doors closed and block out the rapid flooding.

Wading through the eerie lobby, a dim light outlined the room. I could make out the faint outline of a counter and possibly a lamp. It was placed near the center of the floor. Maybe a dozen feet behind it, was a set of treacherous-looking steps which led to the second floor. Four potted plastic plants were set in the corners of the room. Cobwebs and stringy patches of mold clung to their drooping leaves.

There were two other wooden doors, one east and one north. The northern door was held slightly ajar by debris. Nothing but inky darkness could be seen beyond it.

Other than the wind and the sound of the rain pounding against the door, the room was silent, absent of any life. Or perhaps they spied on me from the bordering shadows.

I didn't know or care at that moment as I clawed my way onto the top of the wooden desktop and passed out, shivering and exhausted.

The last thought I had before restless sleep took me — maybe this was all a horrid nightmare. It was as if Death itself had checked in before me, taking Life and Light from this world, leaving me in his wake to witness his handiwork.

FUTURE STORY CONTENT TO BE CONTINUED ON:
AUTHORDEREKBARTON.BLOG

## ABOUT THE AUTHORS:

### DEREK BARTON

**Derek Barton** grew up in northeast Indiana. The typical introvert kid; closer to books than people but grew up with a fascination for horror novels (Stephen King, Dean Koontz) and medieval fantasy (Piers Anthony, R.A. Salvatore).

In April of 1996, he moved to Phoenix, Arizona to find his own path.

He has been married to his wonderful wife, Erika since October 5th, 2012. They have three children, Jenna, Johnny, and Jessiena. And little Rudy, the first grandchild, joined the family in January, 2023!

More content can be found on the official author website, *authorderekbarton.blog!*


## ALSO BY DEREK BARTON:

*Available for sale on Amazon.com, Audible and Kindle!!*

*Consequences Within Chaos (2016)*

*The Bleeding Crown (2018)*

*In Four Days (2017)*

*Elude -- Part One, Part Two, Part Three (2018 - 2019)*

*The Hidden (2019)*

*Evade -- Part One, Part Two, Part Three (2020)*

*Days of Hell & Horror (2021)*

*The Hidden Within (2022)*

*The Infernal Eternal (2022)*

*The Flight of The Dirithi (2023)*

*The Lineage of Prophecy: Pawns & Pieces (2023)*

*The Lineage of Prophecy: The Deity Staff (2023)*

**COMING SOON:** *The Lineage of Prophecy: Beyond the Barrier (2024)*

# BRIAN GATTI

*Brian Gatti was born in Brooklyn, NY and grew up in Manalapan, NJ. He moved to Phoenix, Arizona in 2002 where he lives with his wife Michielle, his son Maxwell, his daughter Annabelle, and his dog The Dude. Brian's son Alex lives with his mother in Jackson, NJ.*

*Brian has a Bachelor Degree in Business Management from the University of Phoenix and an MBA from Thunderbird School of Global Business. When he's not writing or hunting for jobs, he spends his time with his family and thinking about new stories to write.*

T.D. BARTON

T.D. Barton was born in Indiana in the 1950s. He acquired a love of books and for writing at an early age. He has two sons by two marriages: Derek, the oldest who lives in Phoenix and Alec who lives in Palm Bay Florida.

The author now resides in Florida where he divides his time between fishing, painting, writing and composing music.

**ALSO BY T.D. BARTON:**

*Available for sale on Amazon.com, Audible and Kindle!!*

*The Hidden (2019)*

*The Hidden Within (2022)*

*The Hidden: TRIBES! (2023)*

*Graves of the Alien Dead (2023)*

**COMING SOON:** *A Nightmare in Glades County (2025)*

Made in the USA
Coppell, TX
24 January 2025